PINTOS

By Kelsey Day Marlett

Dedications

For Barbara Berk, who inspired me

Marlin Cwach, who stuck with me

David and Emily Marlett, for believing in me

and Tim Hegemier, for giving me the insistent push I needed to finish.

Introduction

"I have stumbled across a very exceptional book this past week. It was so good and written so well, that I absolutely could not put it down! I sped through it at lightening speed, and then it was so good, that now I've started reading it again. It's not unusual for me to read books more than once, but normally I wait a month or two before doing so.

The book is: Pintus by a stunning young author, Kelsey Day Marlett. This astounding girl is only twelve years old and let me tell you something, I've read a LOT of books in my seventeen years - in fact, it seems as though the only time I'm not reading is when I'm writing. That being said, I have never come across a book with so much potential. If I hadn't known that Marlett was twelve prior to reading her book, I would have thought an adult wrote it. The style is impressive and the way she phrases things sticks with you. (You know those days when a random sentence from a book gets stuck in your head because it's so good - read this book and that very thing will happen!)

Pintus is an adventure novel about a young prince who is being ordered to find a princess. Instead, what he finds is a deep, mysterious past with a lot of unanswered questions! The way Marlett writes this will keep your attention - and then ending scenes will blow your mind! The way she writes action will make it near impossible to put down the book!

I highly recommend this book to anyone who loves a good, exciting, fast paced, thriller-action-adventure novel! The characters will immediately find a way straight into your heart. It's one of those books you can't read just once.

Marlett is my new favorite author. She is so young, so inspiring, and show sooooo much promise in the writing world. I cannot wait for the day she is famous, and if my gut feeling is correct, I won't have to wait very long."

- Kya Aliana, author of *Sly Darkness*

Coffee Shoppe

Frost glittered in the glass windows and an icy wind nearly knocked people hurrying through the narrow streets off their feet. The cobblestone road was littered with drifting snow and crusty frost as well; occasional sheets of ice caused browsing people to lose their balance and crash wildly into the nearby wall of some store or stand.

A single cloaked figure was sidling along the walls, darting back and forth in the shadows and barely avoiding the prying eyes of others. His face cast in shadow, the figure made his way to a cozy brick building with a rectangular sign swinging above the doors reading "Coffee Shoppe". Through the glass doors anyone could see the comfortable tables, warm coffee, and lots of older women. The women were all seated together at one table, and of course, they were gossiping. That much seemed obvious, considering the little sparkle in their elderly eyes and reckless look on their faces. The figure opened the door and slipped inside.

After a moment of thought, the figure took a chance and went up to the counter, a coin jiggling in his pocket.

The cloak was stiff from the cold, snowflakes sprinkled over its fabric like the light dustings in the pedestrians' hair outside. He reached up and set the single coin on the counter. "One coffee, please." He paused. "And. . .extra milk and sugar."

The worker nodded, his flour-smeared apron sliding up and down on his chest. The figure, guessing that he had a while to wait before his coffee would be ready, chose a corner near the gossiping women and eavesdropped.

"Jeannette, we all know you weren't once married to a king," snickered one of them. She paused, a sneaky smile on her face, and leaned forward. "Although, if you must know, the prince and I are very close friends."

If the cloaked figure had had a drink, he would have sloshed it all over himself in surprise.

"What, that eleven year old boy of a prince? Prince Pintus?" another woman inquired.

"The very one," she said, nodding knowingly.

"Yes, I'm so sure," said Jeanette sarcastically. "You must be great friends with that eleven-year-old boy, I'm positive. But I know everything about that boy, everything. For example, I know that he has a *pigeon* that he carries about on his shoulder."

"A pigeon!" laughed the second woman as the others gasped in delight at the juicy bit of news. "What utter nonsense. He carries about not a pigeon, but a rat!"

"A rat!" shrieked another woman, looking as though Christmas had come early. All of the women leaned in, eyes wide and amazed. The figure fidgeted slightly.

"A rat," said the second woman calmly. "And not only that, but he feeds it at the table, with his family right there. I've heard it loves salmon."

The figure couldn't stand listening anymore. He ran to collect his coffee, and then retreated outside in the frigid air again. Slowly he took a small sip of the sugared coffee, and as it warmed his insides, he pulled off his hood in the safety of the dark shadow.

"I," he said heatedly, "do *not* carry a rat around!" He reached beneath his cloak to retrieve a tiny golden-brown saw-whet owl, who gave a chirp of agreement. "And I," he continued, replacing the owl beneath his cloak on his shoulder and looking up towards the castle, "*never* knew that old lady!"

He despised people lying about other people, but being the prince of the kingdom, he couldn't expect anything less. Everyone expected marvelous things from him, the son of the greatest king ever known. However, he just wanted to leave the confinements of the castle, wanted to for once be treated as an equal. He had more freedom than anyone in the entire kingdom . . . and yet he had none.

He replaced the hood. Prince Pintus, that was his name. Prince Benjamin Pintus Sacco, the son of the great and mighty King Ericson Horace Sacco. Endlessly he had thought to himself, *Why have I such an odd name? Why can't I have a name like Harry, or John, or Billy? Why Pintus?* But that was his name, and he had come to accept and even like it.

He glanced at the clock tower in the distance. Misty, distant clouds were twisted around the tall tower. It was four o'clock in the afternoon. Immediately alarmed by what he saw and realizing that he was cutting this one dangerously close, Pintus set off at a run towards the castle, black cloak billowing out behind him.

Four thirty-five, four-forty . . . Pintus's legs ached as he tried to increase his speed even more. When he finally reached the moat filled with scaly crocodiles which had been trained to adapt to the freezing winters, he sent up eight shrill whistles. After the eighth whistle, he waited, shifting from foot to foot uneasily and impatiently.

Several seconds later, the wooden drawbridge was heavily lowered and Pintus ran across it to start up the winding stairs to the meeting room.

He threw off his cloak, revealing his regal clothes for meetings such as the one he was late for and making his tiny owl immediately visible as well. The tiny bird shrieked and bolted off to streak after him instead of wobbling on his shoulder. Pintus kept running, eyes scanning the hallways for the door leading to the meeting room and wondering what time it was. His breath came in gasps as he struggled up the many stairs, knowing that all probability pointed to his being completely and inexcusably late. Finally, he reached the eleventh floor and collapsed against the door, wheezing and gasping.

When his breathing finally slowed back down to a normal rate again, his owl settled onto his shoulder and he eased open the door.

Pintus found himself standing before a group of men all dressed in tight black suits and one woman wearing equally somber attire, all of them looking at him with the same disapproving glower.

"You're here," said one of them darkly.

"Twenty minutes late," added another.

King Horace was sitting at the head of the sleek brown table which Pintus knew servants had spent hours polishing, his pure golden crown resting comfortably on his head. He had a round face with brown eyes and a friendly beard growing from his chin.

As he always did at the sight of his father's beard, Pintus wondered how anyone could be able to stand having a beard like that, always getting in the way of things and drooping into his food. Who would want something as trivial as hair sprouting off your chin to get in the way of things?

"I am quite sorry for my lateness," said Pintus. "I was studying the language of the kingdom and became . . . carried away in my interest." He avoided his father's eyes, knowing very well that King Horace knew him well enough to know that he would never become carried away in his studies.

"I see," said someone else.

Pintus looked over in the direction of the voice and recognized the speaker as the only woman at the meeting. She had high-tied hair and a lined face. Pintus silently pondered how his father could possibly have had enough trust in her to allow her to attend.

"Well, do join us at once." She was looking at him with suspicion, something that immediately made Pintus think regretfully how unkempt he must have looked, blotchy-faced, out of breath, and with streaks of dirt on his clothing and face. He sat at the other end of the table, eyeing them nervously, his owl ruffling its feathers restlessly.

"So, as to the reason we have gathered here today," said King Horace, clearing his throat. "We are here, as Prince Pintus might have guessed, to discuss his future.

We thought it only fair that you be present, son, although I must insist that you keep silent."

Keep silent, when the meeting was about *his* future?

"Yes, Father."

"Very good. Now let us begin. The Prince's birthday is tomorrow, and he shall be turning twelve years, one year away from thirteen. Thirteen is only one year away from fourteen, and fourteen is only one year away from fifteen. Fifteen is the year by which he must have found a suitable bride, because at age eighteen, he is to be married and begin his training as king. Therefore, since he is soon to be twelve, and twelve is only one year away from thirteen, and thirteen is only one year away from fourteen, and fourteen is one year away from fifteen, by which time he must have found someone, he should begin searching for a suitable bride now."

What complete nonsense, Pintus thought angrily. *I'm eleven years old and am expected to be looking for my queen already.* He stopped. No. No, he was the prince of the kingdom, and he had a responsibility. He would have to stop griping and just bear it out. He took a deep breath. He was lucky, probably the luckiest boy alive in the entire kingdom. He had a warm, comfortable bed, a wealthy family, and about forty servants available to him at the snap of his fingers. The lack of freedom hardly mattered in the great scheme of things, right? So many boys would kill for his position, so many people would do anything for his –

"Don't you agree, Prince?"

Pintus looked up, jolted out of his thoughts. "What?"

King Horace gave him a cold glance. "I said that Princess Hannah seems suitable. Wouldn't you agree?"

Pintus's stomach contracted. "Princess Hannah?"

King Horace looked at him sternly. "Princess Hannah, from the northern kingdom. If we were to join you two by marriage, we would be able to unite our kingdoms and gain more land."

Pintus felt as though his insides had been sucked out. He didn't even know Princess Hannah. She had attended several events in the royal community but had never spoken to him. All he knew was that she had pretty, long red curly hair that flowed all around her shoulders and delicate green eyes. How could someone he didn't even know be suitable?

"I haven't met her," said Pintus softly.

"Does it matter?" sniffed the woman with the high-tied hair. The way she said it made it obvious that the only answer was no.

"No, ma'am," murmured Pintus.

"I didn't think so," she said icily.

King Horace looked at Pintus as though he had deeply disappointed him. Pintus shifted uneasily and avoided eye contact.

There was a moment of tense silence, and then one of the suited men glanced at his watch and tapped it as though he was deeply saddened by what he saw. "I am afraid I am already running late for another meeting, my fellows," he said. "I thank you deeply for inviting me for this meeting concerning Prince Pintus's future." He stood and bowed respectively to King Horace and then to Pintus.

As though taking this as the cue, everyone else filed out, bowing to both of them before leaving. The woman with the high-tied hair gave Pintus a disapproving look, shaking her head and mouthing to herself, *Boys and their pets*, eyes focused on his owl, before striding smartly out of the room.

Finally, it was just Pintus and his father. They stood in silence for several seconds, and then the king asked, "Why were you late, Pintus?"

Pintus silently relished in his father calling him by his first name and only his first name. Guilt swelled in his chest.

"I already told you, Father," he said. "I was studying my kingdom's culture and lost track of time."

"Pintus." King Horace spoke with a firm voice. "Tell me the truth, and tell it to me while looking me straight in the eyes."

Pintus looked carefully into his father's eyes. He had much – too much, in fact, practice in inventing stories for why he had been late for something. "Father, I was late because I became carried away in my studies."

King Horace seemed to know that Pintus was not being completely honest, but if he did, he didn't show it, for he was a man of trust. "All right, thank you for being honest with me, son." He paused. "You are excused. I shall send four servants to wash and clothe you. I expect you to be in bed by eight fifteen. I will have another servant check in to make sure you are settled for bed. Please remind one of them to send two guards outside your windows. Be ready tomorrow for your birthday celebration."

He lingered by the door. "And, son," he said, "do be sure to enjoy yourself tomorrow."

And he stepped out, leaving Pintus alone with his owl to grapple with his thoughts.

Thief

When Pintus opened his eyes the next morning, a buzzing excitement related with his birthday twisted in his stomach. Well, he was twelve. He tried unsuccessfully to push away the immediate thought that swam into his mind every morning of how to sneak out of the castle again. Several seconds elapsed, then Pintus gave in and allowed himself to consider the possibilities of how he would slip away, the excuse he would use, etc., etc. . .

In the semidarkness, two round little yellow eyes blinked open. Pintus smiled. "Cleven, you're awake."

It had taken Cleven nearly three years to learn and adapt to human sleeping patterns. Cleven darted up and rested on Pintus's forehead. Only the size of Pintus's fist, Cleven was soft and comforting to have there. Pintus reached up to stroke the small bird, and Cleven gave a gentle sigh of contentment in response. Pintus let him rest there for a moment, and then muttered, "Are you up for something to eat?"

Cleven swiveled his head back and forth and crawled down onto Pintus's shoulder.

Pintus smiled. "Good. Me too."

He reached his arm out from beneath the sheets and picked up a polished silver bell. The cool metal against his fingers, he rang it once. The sound was clear and sharp, echoing throughout the castle halls. He rang it a second time and finally a third time, and then set it down on the cabinet next to his bed again. Silently he counted, *one, two, three, four –*

"Sorry we took so long, Your Highness." Three servants scrambled into the room, two carrying royal clothing and one with a plate of food. "And may we wish you a healthy twelfth?"

Pintus nodded curtly and they began to dress him. Cleven remained on the pillow of Pintus's bed, watching calmly with wide bright eyes.

"The usual cloak today, Your Highness?" one asked. Pintus nodded. They dressed him quickly, then served Cleven and him fluffy pancakes and brilliantly yellow scrambled eggs with specks of spices. A fork, knife, and spoon were set neatly next to the food. Cleven flew over at the sight of food. Birthday breakfast.

"Please hurry, Your Highness," urged one of the servants. "Today is your birthday celebration, and you must be ready by three o'clock."

Three o'clock? He had plenty of time. Enough time to. . .

". . .afraid no pets are allowed in."

"Excuse me?" blurted out Pintus, jiggling his shoulder so Cleven swayed. "No pets are allowed into my own birthday celebration? But what about Cleven?"

"I'm afraid we will have to take care of him today, Your Highness. It's all been arranged by the king. Cleven shall be in good hands with your service workers." The servants preferred to call themselves service workers, as though it were a more dignified term for their employed position.

"What nonsense!" complained Pintus. "Cleven is my friend and he shall attend my celebration."

"With all due respect, Your Highness, it is quite too late for that now. Everything is in order, and we don't plan to change it."

Pintus gave them a look of deep contempt. "You are excused."

Looking as though he might want to say something else, the servant left without a backwards glance. Pintus held his cloak, probably the only article of clothing he did not wear regularly, and battled with his thoughts. He could go to the Coffee Shoppe again.

But for what? To listen to old women gossiping about him? Or he could buy some fruit, maybe a peach. He loved peaches. But how to eat it? They weren't sold smoothly cut out and seedless. They were sold in strange sphere-like shapes. The outside was unnervingly fuzzy. He had watched them being sold, and even seen a little boy sink his teeth into one, fuzz and all. Juice had squirted all down his front, and the boy didn't even flinch. He just kept eating. But the fuzz and imperfectness made Pintus unsure and nervous. No, he wouldn't get fruit.

"I like the Coffee Shoppe enough," he murmured to Cleven. "And I have until three o'clock. Let's go down there, get some coffee, and explore around a bit." He held out a piece of egg to Cleven, who delicately picked it up in his tiny talon and ate it. "What do you say?"

Cleven chirruped.

"Great. We'd better go meet the front guard."

Pintus made his way down the castle hallways leading to the stairway in a combination of darting into the shadows and pressing himself against walls as he went. His heart pounded as he watched royal cabinet members pass by, talking in low secretive voices.

Pintus plucked Cleven from his shoulder. "Go tell the front guard I'm on my way," he advised. "I'll be there soon, but he may as well have a warning so he'll be expecting me." Cleven immediately jumped off Pintus's finger and was off, just a tiny blur to human eyes.

Feeling slightly reassured now, Pintus kept moving until he found himself on the winding staircase that led to the moat. Knowing there was little chance of anyone being on the staircase, he ran down, taking the steps four at a time. He kept running in tight twists, not even noticing that he was beginning to lose control. It wasn't until he lost balance and smashed down face first on the steps below that he decided to take more care going down. With his chin bleeding, elbows grazed, and eyes watering, he gingerly walked down the rest of the way, carefully clutching the railing.

"Your Highness, you're here," a voice said at once as Pintus dragged himself out and into the grassy area next to the castle. His chin hurt and he already felt like turning back, but he drew himself to full height and looked with dignity to the front guard.

"I am," said Pintus, and accepted Cleven from the formally dressed, soft-eyed guard. "And I am ready to go." He tightened the cloak around himself.

"Listen, Your Highness," said the guard, voice suddenly going quiet and motioning for Pintus to come in closer. Pintus leaned forward. "I strongly suggest you do not go out today." The guard's voice was low and serious.

"Why not?" questioned Pintus.

"There is . . . a danger," murmured the guard. "And I think it might be . . . plotting something. I know this sounds crazy, but I think something very terrible is going to happen. Soon. I think you need to stay in the castle, where there are servants to protect and –"

"Thank you, front guard," interrupted Pintus. "I appreciate your concern for my welfare. However, I must insist that I go today. I promise to be extra careful."

The guard looked hesitant, but no one ever argued with Pintus. It was law. He stepped aside, and the drawbridge clattered down so Pintus could go across. He pulled the hood over his eyes, and ran over, feet making thuds on the wood as they hit the ground. A crocodile snapped its jaws at him as he passed, and Pintus's heart jumped momentarily. To the village!

The village was particularly crowded today. People swarmed along the cobblestone roads, and children were squealing and running about. *Could that be me?* Pintus thought every time another wild boy ran past him, shrieking and giggling. Finally, he made it to the Coffee Shoppe. Thinking of the inside warmth and comfort, Pintus was reaching for the door handle when he heard something behind him.

"Let me go, you monsters, I didn't do anything wrong!"

Pintus turned around. He felt Cleven shift on his shoulder. Two heavily armed guards were struggling with one enraged screeching girl that seemed around the same age as Pintus.

"Shut up! Shut up now, and get in the cart," one of them snarled.

The girl twisted around, peering hatefully at the wooden cart with barred windows that awaited her. From behind the scene, a broad, older man with gray stubble on his chin cried triumphantly, "This'll be the last time ye steal somethin' from *me*!" It was the man Pintus had seen selling fruit.

Pintus turned around. It . . . it was none of his business. There wasn't anything he could do. If that girl had stolen something, then it was her fault for breaking the law and getting caught. *Thieves are thieves.* But no matter what his brain told him, Pintus couldn't shake off the feeling that the girl was innocent. His fingers had gone numb from holding the cold metal door handle for so long. He snatched it back at once, rubbing his white fingers vigorously and pounding them under his armpits, using that as an excuse to continue watching the scene unfold.

The girl was fighting terrifically. Her dirty black hair, grimy face, and small skinny frame gave the impression of weakness and hunger. Instead, she was throwing those bony legs out in every direction, howling and delivering impressive blows to both guards who firmly kept an unreasonably hard grip on her arms.

His fingers warming again, Pintus grasped the handle and was opening the door when he heard a thud. The girl cried out in pain. He froze. *They must have hit her,* he thought, and a sudden rush of hot blood surged through him in anger. What kind of an animal would hit a girl? Cleven had tensed too, and before he was fully aware of what he was doing, Pintus wheeled around to face them.

"Release her at once!" he thundered, bolting forward and yanking down his secretive hood.

The guards laughed. They *laughed.* "Oh, and I suppose you think we'll listen to you because you pulled down your hood?" chuckled one of them.

"Big, dramatic moment!" howled the other.

Feeling cheated and annoyed at their disregard, Pintus realized these guards must have been in the lower class of servants and had never before been given the honor of seeing the prince. Pintus could hear his heart furiously banging in his ears. But as the guards laughed, they had loosened their grip on the girl.

Both the girl and Pintus realized that at the same time. Pintus dove forward into the guards' arms, and the girl used every bit of her strength to yank away from them. Cleven shrieked and flew from Pintus's shoulder as they wrestled the girl free. Finally, their combined strength snapped her free from the unprepared guards. The girl was off like a lightning bolt.

Pintus paused for a moment as she disappeared into the crowd, and then suddenly two powerful, rough hands struck forward and shoved him from behind. Hard. Pintus had never before been even touched by anyone other than Cleven or his father, and so as he sprawled forward onto the snowy ground with only his bare hands to catch himself, he was too shocked to speak.

"Just who do you think –?!" the guard yelled, slashing up a club above his head.

"Leave 'em, Lanks!" came the other guard's voice from behind him. "We got a more important crime over here! And hurry – he's about to get away!"

Pintus watched, terrified, as the guard pulled back his club. He didn't say anything more to Pintus, but the hatred in his eyes was message enough. As the guard strode off, Pintus waited until he was out of sight, and then slowly stood, quivering.

Cleven immediately soared back to Pintus and out of sight beneath his cloak, looking equally shaken. There was snow smudged onto his cloak now, and his sleeves were soaked from catching himself in the ankle-deep snow. His injured chin ached as he, at long last, entered the Coffee Shoppe.

Since his own guards hadn't recognized him, Pintus didn't bother pulling his hood back up as he bought himself a sugary coffee and sat down at a small table. Cleven, on the other hand, remained beneath his cloak to avoid attracting unwanted attention.

As he took a couple sips of his hot drink, his mind began to catch up with his actions.

What have I done? Pintus already felt regretful and angry at himself. All his justifying thoughts for his actions dissolved. He had helped a thief. Why did he have to go and do that? What kind of fool would rebel against his own government? It wasn't like he was going to get a medal for "Helpful Friend" or be given a "Good Decisions" award, *that* was for sure. For all he knew, the girl could've been lying through her teeth when she had cried out that she hadn't stolen. And yet he had helped her, helped a complete stranger. Pintus avoided his guilty feelings and tried to drink his coffee, but his mouth felt rubbery and the coffee didn't do him much good.

"Hey you."

Pintus turned around, wondering what could happen now, and gave a jolt of surprise, nearly sending coffee splashing down his front. The girl, the dirty-haired, grimy-faced girl was standing there, barefooted and bony.

"Ack!" Pintus yelped, trying to stay quiet so no one would turn around and look. Cleven's little claws dug into Pintus's skin in surprise at Pintus's cry. "Ouch. I mean, what – what are you doing here?"

"I just wanted to say thanks. Can I sit?"

Pintus nodded weakly. She sat and raised her arms to rest her elbows on the table, face curious with a slight flicker of suspicion deep in them, as though she didn't trust anyone. He noticed for the first time that her eyes were ringed with small dark circles.

"You helped me," she told him.

"Yes," Pintus muttered.

"You don't even know me," she pointed out.

"I'm aware of that," Pintus responded.

They looked across the table at each other for a long moment, and then Pintus asked, "What's your name?"

The girl responded with an angry voice. "*That's* none of your business!"

Pintus was surprised that one minute she was hinting towards her being thankful that he had helped her, and now she was shouting at him, so he quickly tried to cover up his mistake. "Okay, okay," he said anxiously, realizing people were looking up at them. He tried to ignore his slight irritation at someone refusing to answer his question. "That's fine. But I *need* to know the truth: did you steal the fruit or not?"

The girl was quiet for a moment. "I didn't," she said finally. "Not really. I found a peach on the ground, and I don't have the money to – and I . . . I didn't feel like buying lunch yet, so I picked it up and took a bite. Then that maniac pounced on me and started shouting and waving around a zucchini."

"A zucchini?" Pintus laughed.

"A zucchini," said the girl, looking dead serious. "He got me a couple times too, here, look at this." She held out her arm and showed him a red welt in the exact shape of a zucchini, or maybe a cucumber. Pintus struggled not to laugh.

"I see," he managed. He was having difficulty in telling whether or not she was joking.

The girl relaxed slightly and leaned back in her chair, looking silently at Pintus's coffee as he raised it to his lips. Pintus found it a fascinating mystery, not to know the girl's name. When the prince asked for someone's name, it was given. But it comforted him to know that his identity was unknown to her as well, and he figured that she must have felt the same way. He opened his mouth again, then shut it. It wouldn't do any good to ask her anything else, and he knew it.

After several seconds of silence, the girl stood up. "I just – thanks. I need to go." She turned to leave, and then paused. "And by the way," she said, a slight smile curving up on her face, "Happy birthday."

Celebration

Dressed in delicate black clothing, his brown hair combed neatly, and with (after quite a lot of persuading) Cleven resting proudly on his shoulder, Pintus stepped into the ballroom in the castle, still wondering how on earth the street girl had known who he was and that it was his birthday. No other phrase than "happy birthday" was necessary. He knew immediately that the girl knew his secret, and that he would have to trust her to keep it.

"Ah, Prince Pintus, you have arrived!" said a tall, suited man with a wise face and gray hair.

Pintus's heart sank. It was his advisor, Mr. Cane, and he was probably about to launch into a discussion about the dangers and responsibilities of parties and being twelve years old. Pintus tried to scramble away before Mr. Cane could get to him, but the man was hovering at his side within seconds.

"Your Majesty, I must wish you a safe, happy birthday!" he boomed, reaching out and clasping hands with Pintus. Already uncomfortable, Pintus gave a little whimper.

"I see you have brought your owl," said Mr. Cane, an obvious note of disapproving in his voice.

"Yes, Mr. Cane," replied Pintus, attempting to worm his fingers from Mr. Cane's.

"I also see you are wearing a most handsome suit and look as grown up as ever, like a man already. On the topic of men, I was recently speaking to your father about a new law we are considering which concerns the alcoholic beverages the commoners have been consuming. Do you find it fair that we should limit the amount of alcohol people may drink?"

"I – I figure it's their choice," said Pintus, taken slightly aback at the question. "If they choose to abuse the privilege and make unwise decisions, then it's their fault, and we shouldn't have to worry about it unless it's affecting other people. Um, Mr. Cane," he added, looking around, "where is everyone?"

"Your guests will be here soon enough," Mr. Cane grunted. "In fact – look!"

An orchestra was assembling on the stage, and people were setting up tables and were decoratively arranging biscuits and other yummy foods.

"They are to arrive at one o'clock sharp," continued Mr. Cane. "Right now it is twelve forty-seven, so everyone will be here to celebrate your aging in exactly twelve minutes."

"Wonderful," said Pintus, trying to sound enthusiastic as Mr. Cane cycled back to the conversation of alcohol.

He watched as the clock on the wall ticked away the minutes, and at last it was twelve fifty-nine. As soon as the last second faded, the entire room began to swell with people and the orchestra began to play. Pintus wished he could disappear in the crowd, but people seemed attracted to his gold crown like moths to a lamp.

A series of girls were following him about, and he found it extremely irritating. Though many, many people were present, there always seemed to be enough space to dance. That was the one part of the party that Pintus found very enjoyable. Old people, teenagers, even toddlers danced on the polished floor, and all of them were having the time of their lives.

Though Pintus knew it to be inevitable, he was not particularly delighted when a pretty brown-haired girl asked him to dance with her. Feeling desperately awkward, he nodded and shuffled onto the dance floor. He had been given dance lessons earlier, but he still felt nervous. He placed his hand on her hip and she grasped his shoulder. They wobbled through the dance steps, the girl continuously looking passionately at Pintus's face until he could hardly bear it and broke away as the song ended.

It was far more enjoyable to watch the dancers than to actually be one of them, Pintus decided as he tried to put as much space between him and the girl as possible. Besides, the fact that Cleven was wobbling on his shoulder through each dance step made it all the more strange and difficult. Several other girls asked him, but he gently refused each offer.

Finally King Horace approached him. "Son," he said, "over there is Princess Hannah. Go and ask her to dance with you."

Pintus stared at him with a mixture of horror and terror.

"Hold yourself high," he advised Pintus as he walked stiffly away to talk to Princess Hannah.

There she was, with the careful green eyes and delicate frame. Oh, how he wanted to just turn away and –

"Greetings, Prince Pintus," she said in a smooth voice as he approached her. Her curly red hair was placed in a high bun at the top of her head. Strings of the hair curled down at her ears.

"Greetings, Princess Hannah," answered Pintus. He felt tense, and suddenly, self-conscious. "How are you faring today?"

"Well," said Princess Hannah. "I am enjoying your celebration immensely. Congratulations on your twelfth year."

"Thank you," said Pintus, and then summoned up some nerve. "Would you care to dance with me?"

Princess Hannah's face pinked slightly. "I would very much enjoy that," she said with a pretty smile.

They walked out onto the dancing floor and grasped hands. A new song began and they started the dance.

"You can tell a lot about a woman by the way she dances," his father had once told him. And as Pintus danced, he could immediately tell that either Princess

Hannah had been taught a different dance style, or he had. They often stepped on each other's toes and stepped in opposite directions. By the end of the song, they were both flushed in the face and frustrated. They separated at once, and Pintus sped off to try to blend in with the crowd again, feeling terrible, as though he had disappointed his father.

As Pintus walked back to his father, King Horace did indeed look slightly put off. He merely said, "Thank you, son," and nodded tightly in acknowledgment.

Partly just for comfort, Pintus took Cleven off of his shoulder and looked at him admiringly, trying to take his mind off his failure with Princess Hannah. Part of him felt relieved that Princess Hannah and he were not good dance partners because he did not feel at all ready to be choosing a queen, and the rest of him felt embarrassed and disgruntled at the whole event.

Thunk.

Pintus paused on his way to a refreshment table, and glanced upwards, where the strange noise had come from. *Thunk. Thunk, skitter, skitter, skitter.* Now several other people looked upwards at the stone ceiling. It sounded as though something was scurrying up the top of the castle. *Thunk. Thunk.*

"Everybody freeze!" shouted a voice suddenly. The orchestra stumbled over their song and the dancers came to a jolting stop. A calm looking guard with a sword belt dangling at his hip held his gloved hand in the air.

"Everybody freeze!" he shouted again.

No one moved. The last note the orchestra was playing swung to a stop.

"We believe there is an intruder attempting to break into the castle," said the guard. "We will begin a search around the perimeter. Please stay calm and do not leave this room."

Someone hollered, "We heard something on the roof!"

Another panicked, "They could be trying to break in from the top!"

Now a slightly alarmed look on his face, the guard demanded, "You heard something on the roof?"

The room erupted into choruses of "yes", and "it sounded like something climbing", "you've got to believe us", and more.

Pintus suddenly remembered, with a stab of fear in his chest, the front guard's words. *There is . . . a danger. And I think it might be . . . plotting something. I know this sounds crazy, but I think something very terrible is going to happen. Soon.*

Pintus crawled out of his giant bed and stood next to the even more gigantic glass window that served as a huge wall behind and around his bed. Cleven, still in Pintus' bed, was fast asleep, and, though Pintus would like to have (he always liked to have) the owl's company, he did not awaken him. He liked this window, because it was cleverly tinted so he could see out of it, but no one could see into it. Pintus leaned against it, and a chill skittered down his spine. The glass was smooth and cold.

As he puffed breath out from his cheeks to make fog on the glass, he thought about the earlier events of the day. After the panic that the guard had made at the birthday celebration, he had come back around twenty minutes later and reported to everyone that it was simply a false alarm, that nothing was amiss, and that what they had heard was simply a branch from an overhanging tree hitting the roof and sliding down it. Pintus could almost hear the crowd's sigh of relief as they all continued the party and at last shuffled out.

After the party, Pintus was to attend another meeting about his future. He did so, and almost the entire meeting was about how Pintus and Princess Hannah had not danced well together, and possible alternative options. Though Princess Hannah had not particularly ever appealed to him, and though he still held the opinion that it was ridiculous for him to already be looking for a bride, he felt a weight of shame that he had not been able to live up to his father's expectations.

"Do not stress, my dear son," King Horace had said to him afterwards. "When I turned twelve, I had much trouble finding a princess with whom I could dance with suitably."

"What age were you when you found Mother?" Pintus had asked.

"Fourteen," King Horace had replied with a gentle smile on his bearded face. "But if I had not begun looking at age twelve, I never would have found her." However, despite his father's comforting words, Pintus couldn't shake the feeling that he had let everyone down.

Pintus leaned his forehead against the cool glass now, and closed his eyes, and wondered where that dirty-haired, grimy-faced girl was now. It seemed extremely unlikely – impossible, almost – that he would see her again, but he wasn't sure if that was a relief or a disappointment.

As Pintus gazed out the window, he noticed that something was trickling from the sky, but was it rain or snow? One of the substances smacked against Pintus's window, and he looked at it carefully. *Snow,* he concluded to himself as he watched the delicate white flake melt on the window. He turned around and looked at his gold crown resting at the foot of his bed. He walked down to it and picked it up in his hands. It was funny how this precious object was worth so very much, almost priceless in value, and yet his owl, whom everyone was always criticizing him for carrying about, had much more meaning and value to Pintus than the crown. He held it for a moment longer, and then set it back down. After brushing his fingers along the window once more, he crawled into his safe, warm bed and fell asleep, Cleven at his side.

Reunion

It seemed like Pintus was always finding himself in the Coffee Shoppe. Though he wasn't always aware of leaving, or thinking about it, he would just naturally go out to the Coffee Shoppe. It became a regular thing for him, a common escape, a daily enjoyment. Even after a particularly exhausting day of tutoring lessons, he would still find energy and time to sneak out and rest himself at the Coffee Shoppe. So it was not particularly surprising when the next day, the day after Pintus's birthday and the day after he had helped the dirty-haired girl, he found himself in the shop with a coffee in hand. *I should be feeling terrible*, he thought as he sipped the hot liquid. *I should feel horribly guilty and ashamed of myself for sneaking out here. But I don't. I feel as though I am doing something good, as though I am doing something sensible and kind for someone else. As though fate is telling me to come here.*

The bell tinkled, signifying someone entering the Coffee Shoppe. Not with much interest, Pintus looked over at the person walking in, and froze. Then, with the swiftness of the owl hidden beneath his cloak, he suddenly stood up, staring in disbelief at the newest arrival. Coffee sloshed in his mug. It – it was the girl, the dirty-faced girl, and she had spotted him too! She immediately made a beeline for the table he was sitting at. Two emotions, panic and excitement, swirled at his insides. She knew his identity, and she was coming to his table. Part of him wanted to dive under the table and hide, while the other longed to stay and talk to the strange street girl. Suddenly he realized that he was still standing, as was the girl on the other side of the table. He sat down with a thump. The girl sat as well, and looked at him with a little smile on her face as though a teacher had just told her she had gotten the right answer. "You're here," she said.

"You're here," Pintus said back. He set down his coffee. "*Why* are you here?"

"Why are *you* here?" asked the girl. "It would be harder for you to get here than for me."

"What makes you say that?" tried Pintus. The girl raised her eyebrows. Pintus's heart sank.

"You know, don't you?" he muttered, watching heavily as the girl nodded. "I had suspected that you knew last time as well, but I . . . I wasn't sure, I suppose. But I need to know – how did you know?"

The girl raised her arms in a noble gesture and brandished them back and forth before miming slinging off a hood. "'Release her at once!'"

"I – it – when – you – it was that obvious?"

"Not to the guards. But when I heard it I had a feeling you were someone who usually had a lot of authority. The first person who popped into mind was the prince, who is just about your age, but I wasn't sure. So after you freed me, I tested you. I said 'Happy birthday' and watched your expression. *Then* it was obvious." The girl grinned. Pintus had to admit, that was smart. But it irked him that he still didn't know the girl's name. She seemed to know what she was thinking, and she said, "Doesn't seem fair, does it?"

Pintus looked at her carefully. "No, it doesn't."

The girl sighed. "I'll answer three questions, you answer two. Deal?" She stuck her hand out, and Pintus tentatively shook it. "All right. You can ask first. I owe you that much." She leaned back in her chair and watched him.

"What's your name?" said Pintus immediately.

The girl seemed to know that question was going to come up, and looked slightly hesitant to answer, but loyal to her promise, she said, "Isabella."

Isabella, Pintus thought. Looking at her, she definitely seemed like an Isabella. A sudden warmth filled his insides and he felt overwhelmingly grateful that now he had a name to go with her features. "Okay. Number Two: I want to know about your family."

"There's really not much to tell," said Isabella, though Pintus saw beneath the toughness a slightly hurt expression deep in her eyes as though she was trying to conceal something. "My father died. I've got Mom, and I've got myself. But that's it."

"Your father died?" Pintus said quietly.

"Yep," answered Isabella, her face masking any emotion.

"I'm sorry," said Pintus blankly.

Isabella didn't respond. "What's your last question?"

"Where do you live?"

Isabella looked like she deeply regretted giving Pintus the chance to ask this question. She looked around, giving the evil-eye particularly to the gossiping women, before leaning in and answering in a low serious voice. "I'll show you," she said slowly and sincerely. "But . . .not now, okay? Later." She looked away. "Now for my two questions. First of all, how and why on earth do you manage to sneak out of the castle?"

"I sneak out with the help of a front guard. He's a friend of mine. I sneak out because I – I guess I get sick of everyone expecting so much and never having any choices, or . . . or any freedom. I know this sounds horribly spoiled, but sometimes I just feel like I need some of those things, I need to be me sometimes, not the High and Mighty Prince Pintus: Son of the Marvelous King Horace." Pintus felt as though a lot of stress had been released as soon as he had come out and said it. He had been thinking along those lines ever since the first time he had attempted to sneak out of the castle.

Isabella was looking at him with a curious expression on her face. "All right. And my second question is the same as your second. I'd like to know about your family."

Pintus let out a whoosh of air. "Where to start?"

"Your mother and father. Trust me, I'm interested; I know basically nothing about the royal family, unlike almost everyone else in the kingdom."

She truly did look like she was curious. It was odd for someone to ask him about his family; most people already knew everything there was to be known about Pintus's family, and more. Isabella watched him carefully as he began to speak.

"Well, my father is King Horace. He's. . .um, a really honest man, I suppose you could say. But he expects a lot from me. He's not the type of person to scream at a guard who makes a mistake, but has an advisor do it for him because he hates upsetting people. My mother, the queen, died when I was a baby. I never knew her." Though he had long come to accept it, he didn't very much like talking or thinking about his mother, or the joy they could have shared together, so he stopped speaking and just looked calmly at Isabella.

Isabella looked back. "Thanks," she murmured.

"Thanks," he muttered back. Wind slammed against the walls of the Coffee Shoppe, rattling the windows and causing Pintus to clutch his warm cup of coffee tighter. He couldn't help but wish that Isabella would show him her home now, but then figured that answering his questions had given her enough discomfort for one day. He drained the rest of his coffee, set the cup down again, and stood up, scraping the chair against the ground.

Isabella stood as well. "I'll be back here tomorrow," Pintus told her. "I'd like to see where you live."

Isabella shifted as though the mere idea gave her chills. "I'll be here." She stressfully rubbed her temples with her slender forefingers. Pintus looked around awkwardly, unsure of what he should say, but Isabella spoke first. "I can't believe this is a prince I'm talking to," she said, and with a truly disbelieving expression on her face.

Pintus shot her an offended look. "Why not?"

"Because princes are supposed to be stuck-up snobs who choose innocent princesses to force into marriage," answered Isabella bluntly.

Pintus felt like someone had whacked him in the stomach with a stick. Was that what people thought of princes? But it wasn't his fault that he was a prince! He

49

waited with a sick feeling in his stomach, scrambling to find a reasonable retort to her statement, but once again she beat him to it. "Honestly, you're hardly any different from regular boys," she concluded.

Pintus raised his eyebrows. "Is that a compliment or an insult?"

"Well, would you rather be a snob or a poor boy?"

Pintus stared at her. "I – a – not all princes are snobs," he insisted. "But just a plain snob – not specifically a prince – but just a snob, then I would say I would rather be a street boy."

"Then it was a compliment." Isabella looked at him wisely. Pintus still felt put off at her unfair judgment, but couldn't resist feeling slightly amused that Isabella would compliment him in such a strange fashion.

She started to head for the door again, and then stopped. "But there is one difference between you and a peasant boy." She nodded at him swiftly and said, "You actually helped me."

Pintus smiled, and Isabella strode out the door. Because he was still thinking of what she had said about princes, he called after her, "I have to say, you sure know a lot about princes, considering that you said you know basically nothing about the royal family."

"Reputation, reputation!" she called back, and the door clattered shut.

Fortune Cookies

As the drawbridge clanged down, the front guard, frantically waving his arms, dashed across it before Pintus could. Pintus stared at him, muscles frozen in place as the front guard lurched to a stop in front of him, an urgent look in his eyes. "C'mon," he said. "We need to go to the *Enutrof Seikooc!*" He looked slightly nervous at approaching the royal prince in such a way, but Pintus didn't mind in the least. "I – when – why?" stammered Pintus.

"I'll explain as we go, but we have to get going, it's an emergency!"

He started running, looking very much unlike his usual reserved self as his long uniformed legs kicked up snow as he ran. "I beg your pardon, Your Highness, but it really is desperately important."

Pintus scrambled with his numb fingers to retrieve Cleven from beneath his cloak. "Go on into the castle, warm yourself and meet me later!" Cleven was off, and Pintus dashed after the front guard.

"I understand completely." Pintus did not say anything about already being freezing cold and that to go back to the village would mean to push against the wind, though his thoughts were definitely along those lines.

As they made their way back to the village, the front guard talked through pants of breath. "The *Enutrof Seikooc* is a Chinese shop," he wheezed as they wound their way through shoppers.

"Is the name of it in Chinese?" asked Pintus, snow fluttering around his face and his cloak billowing out behind him.

The front guard laughed, and then immediately shut his mouth as a nearby boy threw a snowball and it whacked him in the face. He paused for a moment to shout angrily at the boy for his carelessness, and then, with an angry expression on his face and brightly flushed cheeks, he slowed to a walk and answered Pintus.

"No, no. It's 'Fortune Cookies' spelled backwards, and for a reason too. They make the most reliable fortune cookies on the planet, and I mean it when I say that. Whenever I need guidance for the future, I go to the

Enutrof Seikooc. Why bother guessing and hoping when you could get cold, hard fact?"

"In a fortune cookie?" said Pintus incredulously. He had had several fortune cookies before, and all of them had only stupid and cheesy remarks about his future successes or failures, and sometimes even gave ridiculous little pieces of advice.

"Of course. They're so accurate, it's scary. You'll see."

"But why do you need a glimpse into the future? And why are you taking me?"

"Remember what I had warned you about before?" asked the front guard. Pintus nodded, remembering how haunting the words had been about the possible future dangers. The front guard glanced at him and continued. "Well, since the event at your birthday celebration, the situation is getting more and more mysterious. Something just isn't right, and I need to find out what it is."

They reached a tall, forbidding restaurant built of smooth wood painted red, with the words *Enutrof*

Seikooc painted nimbly in black. The front guard

beamed at the shop and opened the door. It was a very

current, very mysterious restaurant with lots of red

swirly carpets and black tables. The front guard picked

out a table and sat down. Immediately a short woman

with creamy- colored skin, shiny black hair, and a red

apron approached them with a notepad in hand.

"Two waters please, and a dozen fortune cookies," the

front guard ordered. The waitress nodded and was off.

"A dozen fortune cookies?" Pintus was amazed. "If

they're so accurate, then why do you need so many?"

"The thing is," said the front guard, "they're not

always accurate about what you're hoping to find out. If

I wanted to know who I was going to marry, and I

cracked it open, it might tell me what I'm having for

dinner tonight. It's correct about that, but it isn't telling

me what I want to know. Do you see the problem?

Hopefully, if we order enough, at least one of them will

give us a hint about the mysterious danger."

Pintus still felt a bit winded at the ridiculousness of it,

but nodded as though he understood. They were quiet,

and taking advantage of that, Pintus leaned back and

looked around. There was a large fish tank with big tropical fish trundling through the water, fat colorful fins making ripples. Pintus silently wondered if they raised those fish to later cook in the kitchen and shuddered as he saw a nearby table receive a plate of grilled fish. Pintus detested all kinds of seafood, something about the smell. He wasn't particularly fond of Chinese food either, except for the sweet crunchy cookies.

The lights all had an exotic twist to them, dangling designs with light bulbs often supported not in the middle but to the side of the wild curves. It was almost entertaining enough to just look at all the wild lights, but still curious, Pintus continued to take in his surroundings.

Most of the workers, of course, were Chinese, and as one of them disappeared into the door leading to the steamy kitchen, he heard them screeching to one another in their language, jagged tones jumping about as they spoke.

Pintus's observations were cut short as the waitress returned, balancing a tray with a plate full of fortune cookies and two glasses of water. She set down the water and then the fortune cookies. "Enjoy," she said, and, as the guard handed her several coins, she left.

"Ready?" said the front guard excitedly. "Which one should we choose first?"

He didn't wait for Pintus to answer. He selected one randomly and bit it open. Pintus leaned over to read it.

A new law shall pass before the month has ceased.

Pintus raised an eyebrow.

"Not unbelievable," the front guard grunted. "Let's move on. Here, you take this one and I'll take this one."

They both snapped open their cookies. Pintus read: *You can't miss what you never had.*

"This is nonsense," grumbled Pintus, searching his mind for something the fortune might be connected to. "Hang on."

You can't miss what you never had.

But that didn't go along with anything in his life. He had never even – wait. *You can't miss what you never had.* He had never had freedom. Maybe that had something to do with it. But he did miss it, and that was what drove him towards sneaking out for it. He crumpled the fortune in his fingers. Though he felt a strange pull to the idea that this fortune might be accurate in some distant way, he couldn't give up the notion that he was right all along: all of those cookies were completely random and unreliable.

"What was it?" asked the front guard as he tossed another fortune over his shoulder.

"Nothing good," Pintus muttered, though silently slipping the thought-provoking fortune into his cloak pocket. "Just 'you can't miss what you never had'."

"Very true, very true," said the front guard, opening a fourth cookie. After looking at him disbelievingly for second, Pintus heaved a sigh and picked another. *The truth lies not in sight, but below the surface.*

Never judge a person by his outward appearance but by his actions and heart.

Objects can be worth much but the value found in live creatures is worth much more.

A situation that may seem impossible to overcome one minute will become your personal triumph the next.

Death is not defeat, but merely your next challenge. Embrace it bravely.

To escape will not satisfy the soul, unless the act of escaping has a purpose.

A day will come when the land shall align in beautiful perfection with all things, good and evil, wise and naïve, indifferent and emotional. When this day comes, you need to rejoice and be grateful for all things.

The last one was so deep and thoughtful that Pintus stared at it for a long moment before he hesitantly crumpled it and tucked it into his pocket, which was becoming crowded with all the fortunes. He particularly liked the fortune that stated "Death is not defeat, but merely your next challenge. Embrace it bravely" because it made death seem different, an old fear with a new spin on it, which somehow lessened his denied and secret fear of it. He did not crumple this one but folded it gently. He still held strong to his opinion about the fortunes, but all the same, he felt a stirring in his gut telling him to save them. Perhaps they would later become a comfort of some kind.

Finally, the front guard said, "These are all excellent, but none of them apply very well to our situation. How are yours? Anything good?"

Pintus shrugged. "Not really. You can read them if you'd like."

He dumped them out on the table.

The front guard sighed. "That would probably be best." So he smoothed out each of the wrinkled fortunes and read them, eyes focused and determined. "Hmm. The only one that looks like it could possibly be something useful is the one about truth lying not in sight but beneath the surface." He reread one of them and slumped back in his chair. "And we have only three cookies left."

Pintus reached over and chose one. "In that case, let's get it over with." He handed it to the front guard who tore it open, and reached nimbly into the cookie to grasp the white strip of paper. He lifted it to his eyes. "'Be the peacemaker, not the fighter, for the fighter never wins in the long run." He groaned before crunching the cookie between his teeth. Pintus picked up the shell of a cookie as well, and ate it. It was very crisp and sweet. He looked at the last two cookies.

"Do you think those last ones could hold the answer?" asked the front guard in a dramatic whisper.

Pintus struggled with himself not to say what he really thought: Probably not. "I – we don't know until we try," mumbled Pintus.

"You're right. Let's just smash both of them at once and get it over with." He took them both off of the plate and set them in front of himself. Then he raised both of his hands, clenched in fists, above them. "Ready?"

"Ready."

The guard flung down his hands, crashing into the cookies and sending flecks of cookies raining through the air like the grains in a sand storm. Both of them leaned in to see the fortunes poking out of the crushed cookies.

Desire is different from and easy to confuse with need.

Remove the log from your own eye before attempting to remove a log from another's.

Pintus sighed. "Why did you bring me out here, front guard?"

"Same reason as I told you," muttered the front guard, looking desperately disappointed. "I regret it, though. All of them are sure to turn out accurate, but I don't think they apply to us yet." He stood up. "Thank you for coming with me, Your Highness. I am truly sorry for the inconvenience."

"No worries, I had a marvelous time," replied Prince Pintus, standing up as well. They nodded politely to the waitress who had come back with a flustered look on her face to clean up the table strewn with unwanted fortunes and empty cookies, and left *the Enutrof Seikooc* to make their way back to the castle. As they stepped out into the cold once more, Pintus slipped his hand into his cloak pockets. He smiled to himself as the fortunes gathered around his hand, creating a sea of paper and ink around it.

Getting There

"No, no, no, Prince, you're doing it all wrong. Look here, at my pencil. See how straight the lines are? Not until they are decently long do you add the branch to it. Okay, now you can write the name." Mr. Cane looked flustered and annoyed. "I don't see why your tutor couldn't have taught you this," he muttered under breath. "Why must I teach this most ridiculous topic just because it is important and proper knowledge?"

Pintus crumpled his paper and picked up a new one. He reached for his quill, sighing to himself, and started drawing his family tree once more, copying it out of a book at his side titled *The King and His Family: The Great Descendants of the Mighty King Horace and More.*

He carefully straightened the lines to make them a good long size before branching them out and writing a name.

"Better," grumbled Mr. Cane, fluttering his fingers about in his pockets to retrieve a handkerchief. Pintus looked at the book with strained eyes, and wrote down in his best handwriting, *Jacob Harrison Sacco.*

"All right, all right now, branch off from him, because he's the start of the whole family."

"Not necessarily," pointed out Pintus, "There's my mother, too."

"No, she is there with King Horace. They pair off together on that branch."

Pintus looked at the paper in the book. "So they do," he sighed. "But . . . Mr. Cane, why doesn't the family of my mother branch out as well?" He had noticed that right after his mother's family line, the page was blank. But between them came Pintus's name. Yet, again there was a blank spot and the rest of the family tree sprouted from nowhere.

"Oh – oh, that's just – that –" Mr. Cane suddenly looked extremely flustered. He mopped at his sweaty face with the handkerchief, and looked at Pintus with wild eyes, his Adam's apple bobbing in and out on his throat like a frog. "That? That's just – just a mistake by the author's hand. The author's, ah, printer printed it, er, incorrectly, you see." Pintus looked at it suspiciously, and brushed his fingertips again the blank spot. It felt pasty and dried. Was that really just blank pa–

"That's enough for now!"

The book was wrenched out of Pintus's grasp, and his paper snatched up. The ink bottle keeled over as Mr. Cane's elbow hit it in his haste.

"I'll call some servants to clean that up!" Mr. Cane said as he went, leather satchel at his side and now completely ready to go.

Pintus jumped out of his chair to avoid the ink and followed Mr. Cane as he hurried to the staircase leading to his office. Mr. Cane pushed his glasses to the bridge of his nose, and still looking flustered and eager to get away from Pintus, said, "Good day, Your Highness, I will be back to continue your tutoring on family trees tomorrow!" and was gone.

Pintus, wondering how on earth he had suddenly wound up alone, without even his owl, wished he could get a closer look at that family tree. He could not conceal the idea of there being something secret and important beneath the pasty smear on that page. Paint, perhaps? Whatever it was, Pintus was eager to discover what was beneath it.

"Coo! Coo!"

Pintus turned around. Up the stairs flew Cleven, no more than a tiny golden-brown streak, making shrieking noises as though someone were smacking him. Pintus hurried forward and extended his arm.

Cleven landed clumsily on Pintus's arm, panting and still shrieking painfully. He ruffled his feathers, ceased his shrieking, and looked at Pintus desperately.

"What's the matter, Cleven?"

Cleven shifted back and forth, and swiveled his head restlessly. Pintus looked at him carefully, wondering why his owl had been squealing so fiercely. "Did someone hit you?" he asked. Cleven kept swiveling and shifting, not answering.

Pintus reached out his left hand and plucked up Cleven from his right hand. Then, holding him firmly with both hands, he inspected Cleven. Nothing looked at all unusual. "Where were you?" Pintus wondered aloud. "You weren't here when I arrived back at the castle."

Cleven's eyes brightened, as though suddenly remembering something, and squirmed wildly from Pintus's fingers.

"Cleven!" complained Pintus as the bird clattered onto the floor, tiny curved claws clicking as he walked slowly but proudly down the hallway. "Where're you going?"

He followed Cleven all the way to the nearest bathroom, where Cleven stopped, and flew up to the door handle. Now feeling annoyed, Pintus said angrily, "Really? Are you serious? You had to use to bathroom?" But Cleven didn't shoo Pintus away to go to the bathroom, instead he vigorously motioned to Pintus with his claws and hopped up onto the counter, looking into the mirror at himself and then flying back to Pintus. Pintus followed him, and standing at the counter, looked at the mirror.

Standing there in the mirror was a young twelve-year-old boy with chestnut-brown colored hair, a smooth white face, and dark eyes so intensely brown that they were almost black.

"What?" demanded Pintus as Cleven pointed at the reflection of Pintus. "There's nothing all that special. You know me. Brown hair, black-brown eyes, pale skin, golden crown. Honest, it's not like there's anything different now."

Cleven motioned towards Pintus's eyes. "Yeah, I know. Black-brown eyes, I just said that. Probably... probably like my mother's were. My mother's . . . and sort like...Isabella's eyes. *Isabella!* We were supposed to meet Isabella! We're late, it's already two o'clock! That's what you were trying to tell me!"

He snatched up Cleven and bolted for the stairs, quickly snatching off his crown and setting it in the usual shadowy corner before jumping down the stairs. Within minutes he was standing before the front guard, wheezing for breath and spitting out between gasps of air, "Put. . .it. . .down. . .I'll. . .be. . .back. . .as. . . soon as. . .I. . .can!"

The front guard nodded loyally, and lowered the bridge. "Be careful, Your Highness!" he called after Pintus as he ran across the bridge.

Pintus yelled back over his shoulder, "No doubt about that!"

When he at last reached the Coffee Shoppe, Isabella was already waiting at the table, fists clenched underneath it. "Where were you?!" she hissed as he sat down hurriedly and tightened his cloak around himself. "I've been waiting all day!"

Cleven popped his head proudly up from the cloak, as to say, "It was all me. I reminded him."

"Argh!" yelped Isabella, springing back in her chair. Several people looked back at their table, disapproving looks on their faces. Realizing that Isabella had never seen Cleven before, Pintus tucked him quickly back under the cloak. Recovering from the surprise, Isabella pointed an accusing finger at the hood of Pintus's cloak where Cleven had jumped up. "What was that?"

"I'll tell you later, shush, shush!" he stressed, looking desperately around to see if any people had seen Cleven as well.

Though still looking slightly suspicious, Isabella let the subject drop. "Are you ready to go?" she asked lowly.

"Ready," Pintus murmured back, and Isabella stood up. She walked confidently to the Coffee Shoppe door, and held it open for him. He grinned. As soon as he got there, she released her hands and let it crash closed. Pintus shot her an irritated look, opening the door himself. "What was the point of that?"

"Sorry," said Isabella in a would-be caring voice. He heard a definite note of sarcasm in her voice. "My fingers slipped."

"I'm so sure," grumbled back Pintus.

"You needed a hint of real life," said Isabella, beginning to wind her way between street vendors and shoppers, but just at that moment an icy white blur of a snowball thrown by one of the young street boys flew and struck her on the face, its cold wet contents slipping down her neck.

Pintus laughed. "Speak for yourself!"

But she hadn't even flinched. Instead she calmly leaned forward, scooped up the remaining snow, and fashioned it into a sphere. Then, looking straight at the boy who had thrown it, she yanked her arm back and reeled it forward, propelling the snowball through the air. It hit the boy squarely in the face, and as he wildly shook his fist at her, she just gave him a smug smile and kept walking. Astonished, Pintus glanced from the boy to her, and thought, *Pretty coordinated, for a girl.*

He didn't say anything to Isabella for several minutes, and she didn't say anything either. The smug little grin on her face said it all, and her smile was enough to make the edges of Pintus's mouth curve up as well. Finally, as they continued down the cobblestone street, Isabella asked, "So, seriously, what was that little bird thing?"

Pintus grinned. "That was Cleven, my owl."

Isabella's eyes widened. "I've heard before from those old ladies in the shop about you carrying around some kind of little animal." She stopped suddenly and glanced around. "Okay, stay close to me," whispered Isabella, and without warning, burst into a run.

Pintus, surprised, ran after her, finding it a struggle to keep up. She had veered off the road and was now darting in between the small gaps in the buildings. Pintus stumbled after her, ignoring the frost soaking through his shoes and the snowflakes resting on his eyelashes.

Finally, Isabella came to the backside of a worn down, rarely frequented store and lifted a board leaning against the back of the brick building. Beneath the board was . . . the wall. No secret doorknob, no hidden entrance at all by what Pintus could see. Isabella leaned forward, and felt nimbly along the brick wall until she reached one single brick. She fingered it for a moment, and then popped it back from the wall, causing it to slide down into the inside of the building. Pintus's eyes widened.

Isabella stuck her hand through the hole formed (if her hand wasn't as bony as it was, it never could have fit) and wiggled it back and forth. Flecks of dust fogged the air so thickly that Pintus couldn't see what Isabella was doing. He cleared his throat, squinted, and as the dust cleared, saw that Isabella had created a suitable passageway. The entrance was unstable and oval shaped.

Isabella turned around to look at Pintus with a little smile on her face and motioned for him to follow her. She lifted her leg over and into the abandoned building. She paused, and looked back at Pintus. The darkness of the store cast her face in shadow.

"Well?" she demanded, impatiently indicating with her hands that he should enter. Pintus looked apprehensively towards the jagged oval entrance. Isabella crossed her arms and looked at him stubbornly. "Are you coming or not?!"

Pintus looked nervously at the entrance, and after a moment of battling with himself, wobbled forward and stumbled in. It was so dark, he couldn't see anything but outlines and figures. He jumped backwards, eyes wide and holding in a silent yell of surprise when he realized that he was nose-to-nose with Isabella. He found himself scrambling backwards, and hitting a grainy, unfinished, wooden wall with cobwebs reaching out at him. He cried out aloud in pain and disgust and lurched away flinching.

Isabella was laughing. "This way," she called.

Pintus clambered in the direction of her voice. He heard her rummaging around for a moment, and then with a scraping noise, a flickering orange flame broke the darkness. For a single second Isabella's brown-black eyes were visible, wide and serious in the small glint of a match, and then the light was lowered to a candle. The flame caught the wick, and Isabella offered the candle to Pintus.

"To hold?" asked Pintus in amazement. His servants *always* held the candle for him.

"Yeah, I'm not about to hold two candles myself!" snapped Isabella, shoving the candle into his fingertips. Pintus grasped it unsteadily, eyes mesmerized by the swaying flame. "It's beautiful," he murmured. He had never really been able to appreciate the full loveliness of a gentle yellow-orange flame flickering so close to him.

"I know," said Isabella lightly, another lit candle in her hands. "Now let's go, Mom's expecting me and I told her that by now you'd be here to meet her!"

She ran in the opposite direction in which they were standing, dangerously, Pintus thought, considering the lit candle she was holding, and disappeared into a room of darkness.

Home

Pintus used his candle to guide himself along the tight-walled hallway until he came to the room into which Isabella had disappeared. He found it increasingly frustrating not to be able to see everything brightly lit as he usually insisted; he almost wanted to call to his servants to light another candle.

But that's more than just spoiled, that's completely rotten, he reminded himself, stubbing his toe and blinking rapidly so the watering of his eyes wouldn't be too obvious. *I mean, I – the Prince! – am here, in the actual kingdom being treated like an equal. And yet, I am silently complaining about not having quite enough light to see perfectly.*

Hearing a loud crunching noise, he lowered the candle so he could see what he was stepping on, and looked nervously down at a piece of crushed stained green glass, which he nimbly jumped over. After one last curve in the hallway, he entered the room.

Isabella was already there, sitting on a cardboard box and her candle set on the dusty floor beside her. Across from her, seated on another box was a slender, bony-faced woman with stringy chestnut-colored hair and dark solemn eyes. The woman was basically wearing rags, but there was a careful dignity about her.

"Mom," Isabella said softly, "this is Prince Pintus."

Pintus slipped into the room, and stared in awe at the woman. She looked . . . familiar, somehow. Pintus tried not to appear too rude as he gazed at her. Her eyes, her hair, her features, all somehow looked familiar. . .

"This is the prince?" asked the woman to Isabella. Her voice was soft and gentle, as though talking about a small puppy. *"Really?"* She sounded almost amused as she said the last part.

"I know it's surprising, Mom, but it's completely true. Trust me, look, he's even got his little owl." Isabella motioned for Pintus to take out Cleven.

Pintus, smiling to himself, reached in his cloak and groped around for Cleven. But there wasn't anything to grab. His fingers went cold. Where was Cleven? He switched shoulders, desperately feeling around. There was no owl to be found.

"He's gone!" he blurted out, trying not to sound too babyish or whiney, though he suddenly felt his eyes burning. "Oh my – oh – Where's Cleven?" He felt as though he was swelling from the inside, and was going to burst any second. Of all times for Cleven to disappear – but he never disappeared. Where was he? Had something happened to him? He felt an increasing panic churning up his insides.

Breathe, breathe, you're all right, you're fine, he just flew off and went back to the castle, he's fine, you're fine. His thoughts desperately tried to comfort him, and after a few seconds of struggling with himself, he gained control.

"I'm sorry," he said primly, though he still felt jabs of panic thundering through his body, "but I left him at the castle before we left because I was concerned that . . . er . . . that he would panic at being in an enclosed area for too long." He gave Isabella a significant look, and she returned it, eyebrows pulled together in confusion.

"Oh, I see. I reckon your owl was in captivity before you received 'im, so now he is petrified of being closed in a cage again, yeah?" The woman gave him a gentle smile. Pintus was once more struck by a strange sense of familiarity.

"Thank you for understanding," said Pintus politely. He paused as he finished speaking, wanting to address her by a name but not knowing what it was.

"I'm pretty good at that," grinned back the woman. "And by the way, you can call me Mrs. Sac– Carole."

"Thank you, Mrs. Carole," replied Pintus. "I really am sorry Cleven isn't here to meet you."

The woman looked at him rather confusedly. "Uh – who's Cleven?" Though she looked puzzled, there was a sparkling warmth to her eyes as she looked at him with a loving gaze.

"I – the owl," said Pintus hastily. "It's the owl's name."

The woman nodded slowly, seeming to understand, the warmth in her eyes still there. She looked almost as though she wanted to hug him. "I see. Well, I am – so, so very glad to meet you. More than you could ever guess."

Pintus nodded back, though he thought it was rather strange for her to be so pleased to meet him. He looked nervously away. Though he silently questioned why she was so happy to see him, he couldn't focus on that now.

He was too completely filled with the fear of Cleven being kidnapped, lost, stolen, or worse. He heard his heart in his ears. Where – was – Cleven? He tried in vain to concentrate as Mrs. Carole began to speak again, but it was almost impossible as he was filled with thoughts of his missing owl.

Mrs. Carole leaned forward slightly, eyes on Pintus, a little smile on her face. "So," she said, "what d'you think?"

"I . . . I don't quite understand your question," said Pintus. Mrs. Carole gestured, waving her arms to emphasize the area around her. "Here, our home. What d'you think of it?" She looked at him expectantly.

Pintus glanced around by the light of the flickering candle. There were no outstretching or branching off hallways. Where was the rest of their – if he could call it that – house? He peered around a bit longer. It was hard to see very well because of the lack of light, despite the weak flames from the two candles. After a moment, he decided to just to go right on and be honest about the dank gloomy room that they called home. That way he didn't have to squint into the darkness and strain his eyes any longer.

"Well, it's hard to say," he said. He looked around one more time. "Where is the rest of it?"

Isabella looked at Mrs. Carole, and Mrs. Carole looked confusedly forward at Pintus. "I don't quite understand your question," she told him, looking a little upset at his question. Pintus motioned to the small, cramped, dusty room around them. "I mean, where are the other rooms and the bathrooms and everything?"

Mrs. Carole said nothing. A minute passed where no one said anything, and then Isabella growled through clenched teeth, "Not everyone can live in a palace, Pintus."

Pintus's eyebrows pulled together. He tightened his grip on the waxy candle, and looked away. There was a long, silent moment. "You mean. . .you don't have. . .?"

"No, we don't," snapped Isabella in a sharp voice that sent the message far more clearly than her words: "Drop the subject. Now."

"Oh. O-okay," said Pintus, trying to sound as though that was perfectly normal and he was completely fine with it, though in truth he was shocked and horrified that some people were living in such conditions. He wondered if he should add that he did indeed like their home even though he was slightly upset by it, but quickly thought better of it and let the awkward subject drop.

Mrs. Carole shifted subjects immediately. "Do you ever find that you have a rather . . . forgive me, please do not take offense at this, a rather unusual, and even odd, name?"

"Oh, that goes without saying," said Pintus with a smile. "But it's out of my control, and I may 's well accept it, right, instead of pouting about it, don't you think?" He tried to assure himself that he was never pouty, but the thought wouldn't come. He had to admit, he oftentimes expected too much. But he was a prince; after all, he didn't know anything else. Until now.

Mrs. Carole looked at him with that lovely warmth in her eyes and a gentle smile on her face. "I very much agree," she said. She spread her arms out openly. "Well, c'mere then," she said welcomingly. Isabella hurried over and nestled next to Mrs. Carole. Pintus just looked at Mrs. Carole blankly, arms limp at his sides.

"Pintus?" said Isabella softly.

"I – I don't know what –"

Mrs. Carole looked at him in amazement. "Hasn't anyone ever given you a hug before?"

Pintus stared at her.

"Well, c'mon over here," Mrs. Carole encouraged. Pintus, feeling extremely nervous, inched over, and as he came closer, Isabella's mother ruffled his hair and gave him a brief hug. It felt surprisingly natural, unlike Pintus's immediate thoughts of breaking his posture and finding himself in an awkward position.

"And thus, the Great and Mighty Prince Pintus receives his first hug," taunted Isabella with a joking smile from her perch on the cardboard box. Pintus backed away, though he felt cozy and warm inside, like a cup of coffee from the Coffee Shoppe.

"It's nice, innit?" said Mrs. Carole. "Nothin' like a nice motherly hug, right, huh?" Pintus nodded silently, avoiding their eyes. It had been nice, but he didn't feel that it was very princely to say so.

"Well, I'm guessing there's some kind of meeting you're late to," said Isabella, standing up and motioning to Pintus to follow her. "We'd better go, Mom." Isabella left instantly and disappeared into the cobwebby hallway.

Pintus turned and looked at Mrs. Carole. He still could not get over the familiarity of the woman. "I – thank you," he whispered.

"Anytime," whispered back Mrs. Carole with a small smile.

Pintus turned and dashed after Isabella, silently agreeing that *yes*, he probably was late for something.

Search Party

The front guard was waiting for Pintus as he reached the front door after clambering off the drawbridge over the moat. He lurched forward and looked at Pintus desperately. "You cannot sneak away anymore!"

He had braced himself against the front door, and was looking at Pintus, dead serious. "You *cannot* sneak away *anymore!*"

"Move aside, front guard," Pintus said stiffly.

"I am quite sorry, Your Highness, but this is desperately important!"

Pintus sighed, giving in as he saw the urgent look on the front guard's face. "Go on."

Looking highly relieved, the front guard said, "You mustn't sneak away anymore, Your Highness, and I'll tell you why: there has recently been a threat to the castle. I was the first to read it, and knew immediately what it was referring to. Here, I still have it." He handed Pintus a slip of paper, who took it with an increasing feeling of anxiety.

Some people believe in fortune cookies. Well, this is not an unreliable fortune cookie. This is true, serious fact. I know for fact that the thing of most importance to the Prince will be taken by twilight tonight, and it will not be given back unless my demands are met in full. You cannot prevent this. There is no point in trying.

"Oh. . .oh, no." Pintus felt himself falling backwards. At once the front guard was there, snatching his hand and yanking him back and away from the moat. Pintus had received death threats and bad wishes from angry and bitter people throughout the kingdom many times before, as it was one of the disadvantages of being the son of the man in power, but this was the first time it had ever caused him any true fear. "Oh my G–, front guard, *Cleven went missing today!*"

He gritted his teeth, trying not to let out any tears. Cleven, his friend and companion, had mysteriously disappeared on the very evening a threatening letter had been found. Without any true thought on his part,

Pintus dove his hand into his cloak pocket and retrieved one of the fortunes he had saved. *Objects can be worth much, but the value which can often be found in live creatures is worth much more.*

He took a deep breath. He had to stay calm, had to be mature. He would have his father send out a search party to look for Cleven. He held tight in his left hand the threat letter and in his right the slip of paper that held the fortune. He carefully tucked away the threat letter into the pocket that wasn't stuffed with fortunes, and turned to the front guard who was looking at Pintus with a horror-stricken look on his face. "It was already taken? The thing of most importance to you?"

Pintus took a deep breath, the fortune clutched in his fingers. "Yes. Let's head into the castle and send out a search party."

"Good plan. I'll have to stay here, though. I'll guard the best I can until you come back. I have a bad feeling about this whole thing."

Pintus nodded swiftly, trying to ignore the waves of nausea that were giving him unwanted pangs of weakness. *No.* He would not allow it – that was this person's whole plan. If he whimpered and was too scared and upset to put anything into action, he would never get Cleven back. It was just some fool who somehow managed to catch him. The thief would be caught before the morning had dawned.

Pintus turned and threw the fortune into the moat. He didn't wait to see if it wetted and crinkled in the water, but wheeled around again and ran for the entrance. He was distantly aware of his feet pounding on the concrete steps that wound up into the castle. When he made it to the first floor, he met a servant.

"Your Highness," said the servant, looking surprised. "What on earth are you –?"

"Where's my father?" interrupted Pintus.

The servant stared at him. "I – Your Highness, with all due respect, you should not be here, you need to be –"

"Answer my question!" hollered Pintus. The servant scrambled over his own words. "He is in the top tower, working on answering questions and complaints from the townspeople! Whatever is wrong, Your Highness?"

"You'll find out soon enough," Pintus assured him, already back on the staircase. He was not aware of feeling at all tired as he sprinted up four more floors, and still with eight more floors to go. He ran into several more servants, but simply raced past them, ignoring their bewildered looks. When he at last reached the top tower and burst through the door to his father's office, his chest was heaving, and he was so out of breath he could hardly speak. "Cleven's missing!" he gasped.

"What?" said the King sharply.

"Father – did you read that letter? The threat one about fortune cookies and stuff?"

"I – yes," King Horace said, paling.

"They actually did it, they've stolen Cleven! He's gone, we need to send out a search party, and immediately!" Pintus looked at him imploringly.

"This is extremely serious," King Horace murmured. "How on earth did they manage it, I wonder?"

"I wish I knew," Pintus moaned, "but we need to send out the search party, and now!"

"All right, I'll be on it immediately," promised the King, standing up, his formal red robe billowing. "You stay here," he added firmly as he strode for the door. Pintus followed him. The king turned sharply. "Whatever you do, *do not leave this room.*"

"What! But –"

"Pintus." King Horace looked at him seriously, and Pintus knew that there was no point in arguing. His heart was banging in his chest. He took a deep breath. He shouldn't have lost control like that. "Yes, Father. I apologize."

"Thank you, Pintus," said King Horace. He left the room, moving at an urgent stride, and closed the door sharply with a snap. Pintus might have imagined it, but he thought he heard the grinding of a lock.

So now he was stuck in a rather small though comfortable room with nothing but a desk inside it while the rest of the castle was preparing to send out a search party to look for Cleven. If this villain were able to capture Cleven, then was it possible for him to kidnap a person as well? Kidnap a servant, attack a guard, assassin a cabinet member? Pintus's gut told him that this was the beginning of something very dangerous, and they needed to put a stop to it before it could heat up into something deadly.

He sat down at his father's desk, and tried to give himself something to do other than think about the situation. At first he tried just to look at the king's papers without touching them or ruffling them out of order, but after a moment he just picked up the stack and flipped through them. The stacks seemed to be ordered by criticism and compliments. Pintus amused himself for a moment by looking through some ridiculous citizen complaints about coffee that burned their tongues and cracks in the road that they tripped over. Pintus laughed aloud when he read a complaint about rocks that were "dangerously placed" and that they stubbed their toes on. After a moment though, even this became slightly boring so he set the papers back down and took out the threat letter.

Some people believe in fortune cookies. Well, this is not an unreliable fortune cookie. This is true, serious fact. I know for fact that the thing of most importance *to the Prince will be taken by twilight, tonight, and it will not be given back unless my demands are met in full. You cannot prevent this. There is no point in trying.*

He could not stop reading and re-reading the message, even though he already had the entire thing memorized, the words etched into his very soul. He drummed his fingers on the polished wooden desk, once again attempting to clear his mind. He propped his elbow up on the desk, and rested his face in his hand.

He couldn't stand just sitting there. There had to be something – anything – he could do to help. Without any organized plan, Pintus stood up and walked over to the door. He grasped the door handle, and pulled. Clank. Rattle. It opened only a crack, but it was enough for Pintus to see the thin yet strong iron chain connecting to the adjacent wall. He had been right. King Horace had bolted the door shut. He was truly stuck in that room. Pintus ran his fingers through his hair, thinking. Finally he went over to the rather small tinted window to the left side of the room and peered out. He gazed down upon the kingdom, the Coffee Shoppe looking like a small square toy from this height. He looked down and saw below him the water-filled moat with the broody crocodiles swimming slowly through the water. Suddenly, a pang of panic shot through him.

The drawbridge had been left down!

"No!" Pintus strained against the glass window. Whoever had plotted this had plotted it well. Now the enemy, whoever it was, had an open door straight into the castle, the very heart of what they were aiming to ruin. How could no one have noticed? He would *have* to put it down, and at once!

Pintus rushed to the door again, and wrenched it. The chain held fast with a clinking noise. With a rush of frustration, Pintus kicked the door. Now with a throbbing toe, a panicking attitude, and a pair of hands crazed to do something – anything – to get out, Pintus was quickly losing control, and he knew it. "Stay calm!" he ordered himself aloud. "Ignore the toe. That was your own fault. Think about your situation logically. The door isn't going to open, and the window is probably a mile away from the ground. Where on earth is the front guard?" He looked in the window's direction. He ran to it and looked out of it, heart pounding. The moat was directly below the window. *Directly below.*

"I must be crazy," groaned Pintus, running over to the desk and ripping the dark thick cloak, that was his father's, off of the chair it had been draped over. He wrenched off his shoes. "I must be completely insane."

The window had a lock on it, but the key was lying right on the king's desk. Pintus took it in his fingers and drove it into the window's lock. He twisted and heard a clicking noise. The lock fell to the floor with a clattering sound. Pintus shoved the window the rest of the way open, doing his best not to think about what he was planning to do because if he thought about it, then he would surely become too utterly afraid to go through with it.

Pintus stuck his head out the window. Though the moat looked terrifyingly far away, there was no denying that it was straight beneath the window. Pintus lowered himself out of the window and onto the slanted roof. He carefully climbed down that roof until he reached the edge, and looked at the moat far below. He ignored the sickening terror that was beginning to creep upon him, and tried not to hear his father's voice saying, "Whatever you do, do not leave this room". His father's cloak, which he had thrown over his own so no one would recognize him, flapped in the wind. He crouched at the edge of the roof, squeezed his eyes closed, lurched forward, and flung himself into the air.

Drawbridge

As Pintus was flying through the air, time seemed to slow around him and he realized what he was doing. His father's image flashed through his brain and his voice rang in his ears telling him not to leave the room. He thought about the sting that he would feel as he hit the water and the crocodiles that churned the water hungrily. As he fell, he tried to keep his posture: *feet down, arms tucked, eyes closed, chin up.* But it was no easy task as the fear began to grip him. No time for fear now, though; he was only feet away from water.

Pintus squeezed his eyes tighter.

Sploosh.

The sting was so powerful that it shot the air Pintus was holding in his chest straight out in a stream of bubbles. He felt himself struggling to breathe, and was immediately thankful for the what used to seem pointless swimming lessons he received at a young age.

The water was so cold he was surprised it didn't freeze him completely. But the temperature of the water was the least of his troubles. He struggled to the water surface and choked down a fresh lungful of frigid air. The two cloaks weighed him down slightly, but he was able to at least keep himself above the surface and swim. He desperately headed toward the earthen bank of the moat so he could crawl out when he saw a thick, scaly green-gray tail whip through the water in front of him.

His heart stopped, frozen in terror.

He didn't move a muscle, but tried to stay at the surface and keep from shaking with cold, all the while the soggy cloaks clinging to his skin and his heart banging so loud he could hear it and was sure that the crocodile could too.

But he didn't have time to indulge in fear. Those traitors could already be sneaking in as Pintus desperately treaded water. Pintus's eyes narrowed.

"Get out of my way, you reptile!" he shouted, kicking his feet wildly and rocketing forward across the water.

He felt something rough brush up against him, and though his flash of courage was still powering him, a rush of fear couldn't help but overwhelm him at that moment. A brief streak of panic overpowering him, he bolted for the edge of the moat and dug his fingers into the earth.

Despite his dangerous situation, he hoped no one could see him in this state, sopping wet and filthy. He threw his foot over the bank top and hastily rolled the rest of him after it. He took a moment, on his back next to moat, to breathe deeply in and out and think about what he had just done. Then, knowing there was no time to spare, he jumped up and ran over to the front door leading into the castle. His body quivered and shook, but Pintus knew there was no way to warm himself until he changed clothing or bathed. All he could do now was pull up his hood to at least protect his identity and finish his deed.

The front guard was nowhere to be seen, and neither were any other guards that might be taking his place. Pintus wrenched open the front door, his fingers wet and slippery, and looked wildly around for the drawbridge crank. To his left the winding staircase towered upwards, but where was the crank?

He was beginning to feel desperate when he found it, hidden in plain sight. It was right next to the door, on the wall next to the door. Thank goodness.

Pintus leaned over, and grabbed the handle. It was now or never. He pushed it forward. *Ugggh,* Pintus groaned, already flushed in the face as the heavy weight lifted a fraction of an inch. The crank was terribly heavy to push and pull. He brought it around in the circle once, a sweat beginning at the top of his forehead. Several times the damp black hood of his cloak fell back and rested on his shoulders, but Pintus wouldn't allow that. Each time he would reach one hand back and pull it up over his head.

After what seemed like a thousand cranks, the drawbridge was halfway up. Energy Pintus didn't even know he had drove him to work even harder, a grim, determined smile of enthusiasm etched across his face.

He kept cranking. He didn't know how long he kept at it, but he continued to crank up the drawbridge with every bit of his strength. Though he was small and weak compared to many of the guards who were paid to do this job, he was making good progress just one crank at a time. As he continued, a rhythm seemed to play out, or maybe it was just that he became bored. But it went *for my kingdom, for my kingdom, for my kingdom.* Crank crank-

crank-crank. Crank crank-crank-crank. Crank crank-crank-crank.

Finally, the drawbridge clanged shut, vibrating up against the walls, and Pintus – soaked, sweaty, and with arms that felt like wet cement – stumbled backwards and fell on his rear-end at the foot of the stairs. "I did it!" he moaned. He had thought his victory would be a bit more triumphant than collapsing in pain and exhaustion next to the drawbridge crank, but nevertheless he was proud of his success. He let himself rest for a couple minutes, occasionally brushing his stiff hair out of his eyes.

"Sssssss!"

Pintus looked up. The snakelike hiss had come from across the drawbridge. Pintus lowered himself closer to the ground so he wouldn't be seen and slowly inched closer to the front door in order to peer out the crack. He searched along what he could see for a source of the noise, eyes flicking along the moat's bank.

"Sssss! I don't understand! It was open!"

Pintus couldn't see where the voice was coming from, but his heart was picking up another wild beat.

"Master will be furious! *Sssssss!* Master will kill the both of us!" snarled another voice.

Pintus desperately yearned to run as fast as he could up the castle stairs where he couldn't hear the voices, where he could assure himself that he had brought up the drawbridge only for safety's sake, and that he was being only paranoid, that he was not actually hearing voices putting evidence with his thoughts. But he was frozen into place, down against the cold floor, water from his hair and cloak dripping onto the concrete.

In the distance came the faint voices of those in the search party, and the nearby hissing voices ceased immediately. Pintus thought they might have gone, but wasn't about to take any chances. He didn't move for several more minutes, and then finally pulled himself up and fled up the stairs and into the castle.

"We sure were lucky this time," said Mr. Cane.

Pintus was sitting in at a council meeting, and they were speaking about yesterday's events.

"Quite lucky that we found the owl – though in bad condition, I must say, still with our animal experts – but really, of all carelessness, we left the drawbridge down!"

"Whoever planned out the whole scheme must have been quite clever, and known our weaknesses," agreed another.

King Horace sat at the head of the table, fingertips together and gazing down at a newspaper. "I could not agree more that we were lucky," he sighed. "Just look at this newspaper." He skidded it across the table so it stopped smoothly straight in front of Mr. Cane. Mr. Cane pressed his glasses up to the bridge of his nose and peered down at it. Pintus leaned over as well to look at it.

Mysterious Hero

SAVES Castle's Wellbeing

The title itself was enough to make Pintus cringe, because he knew exactly what it was referring to. Pintus quickly read the article, heart pounding and guilt surging through him.

After the drawbridge was carelessly left down by the Search Party for the Prince's saw-whet owl, there seemed to be little hope that anyone would notice and alert the authorities. It is believed that whoever had stolen the precious owl had planned for the Search Party to leave the drawbridge down in their haste, and was planning to infiltrate the castle without obstacles. Well, that plan was soon demolished as the drawbridge was mysteriously closed by an unknown cause. Minutes later, a cloaked figure was seen fleeing the area. We believe that this cloaked man or woman was a masked hero willing to risk his or her life by swimming across the moat to pull up the drawbridge, and though we know not the real name of this silent hero, we all give our silent thanks to the humbleness and kindness of this brave commoner.

Article By: Matilda Greenery

"How do they know it was a commoner?" asked Pintus aloud as he finished the last sentence.

King Horace gave him a hard, cold look. "Were you spoken to?"

Pintus looked away. "No, Father."

Even though King Horace did not know that Pintus had sneaked away, he had been more stern towards him lately because Pintus had tended to speak out of turn and lose his stiff, formal posture more often. "Then do not speak back. Do you understand, Prince Pintus?"

Pintus looked at him with guilty eyes. "I do. And I apologize."

"Thank you, son. But to your question: How do they know it was a commoner? They don't. They just know it wasn't someone in the royal family, or someone who serves the castle. So what other choice is there? That goes without saying, that it would be a commoner. And a good, brave commoner too," he added with a thankful expression on his face.

Mr. Cane passed the article back up, and straightened his glasses. "Indeed, we were remarkably lucky, Your Highness. I am just exceedingly grateful for whoever it was that performed this deed."

"And I as well," said someone with spindly spectacles and one eye looking magnified and larger than the other. "I just wonder who 'twas."

"Isn't this new printing press invention simply marvelous?" The man who had spoken pressed his glasses up to his nose and smoothed his graying hair with one hand. "By now, all the kingdom will be wondering about this silent hero. I just wish we had a name to go with the actions."

"It may be better for it to stay a secret," said a man with a rather dreamy look about him and wrinkles etched all over his face. "It makes it more magical this way."

"Magical!" scoffed the woman with the high-tied hair. "*Magical?*"

"Not *literally*," snipped the man. "All of you know exactly what I am meaning."

They all just stared at him blankly.

"I believe I know what our respectable Sir Jester is trying to tell us," said a squat, elderly man with square shoulders and squinty eyes. "To go and brag loudly about the brave deed he or she has done, to go and boast to everyone of the fame he or she may receive for it would make whoever did it seem much less heroic and humble. To go about and shout around to make sure everyone knew of his –or her – ingeniousness would make him seem much less like a silent hero. Do you understand what I am saying? If we were to know the answer to this mystery, it would be a mystery no longer, and the hero would seem like much less of a hero, and therefore have less meaning and value to us."

Sir Jester clapped his hands together, though taking much care to not actually make any noise lest it were to irritate the King. "Precisely, my good Sir Accox, precisely."

Mr. Cane looked as though he understood but wished he didn't. Pintus was looking at all of them with a mixture of confusion and amazement. He had not in the least thought all that through but just wildly done it in the spur of the moment, trying to save his kingdom. He was rather pleased that people were so grateful and delighted at his actions, but he hadn't been expecting all this "silent hero," "mystery person," and "saved by an unknown cause" business. But for now, it hardly even mattered. Cleven was safe – injured – but safe. The castle was safe. The kingdom was safe.

For now.

Visit

Pintus was led by Mr. Cane and a couple men and women in white coats down through the castle. Pintus curled his thumb against his palm to stop his fingers from quivering. "How is he?" asked Pintus, looking at one of the men in white coats.

One of the women answered him, one with brown hair in a loose bun at the nape of her neck and thick brown square glasses. "Improving miraculously. Cleven is quite the patient – most of the animals we serve take at least twice the amount of time that he did to even begin to heal. The only problem is that he seems slightly depressed. We hope that when we bring a friend – you – in there, he will lighten up, because I know – for crying out loud, *we all* know– he missed you."

Pintus regarded her with curious eyes. "How do you know that, may I ask?"

The woman looked back at him with a little smile playing across her face, but didn't answer directly. "You'll see soon enough. He's been making it pretty obvious for us."

Mr. Cane was looking at the woman's careless, sloppy bun and square glasses and listening to her light, commoner's voice with a look of deep disgust and disapproval on his face.

The white coated people slipped in front of Pintus and Mr. Cane in order to open the door for them and with two clicks, both of the double doors were swung wide. "Do follow us, Your Highness," said one of the men in white coats, and walked confidently off into a white tiled and white walled room.

Pintus followed him, curiosity edging him on at a quicker pace. As he looked to the side and around him, he saw many comfortable cages appropriate for recovering animals. Pintus noticed a cat with bandages around its head that was sleeping at the back end of a crate with bars and a badger in a large glass container that had a strap of bandage going over its shoulder. He looked around for a cage containing his small feathery friend, but it was nowhere to be seen.

"Where is Cleven's ca –?" he began, but one of the people leading him cut him off before he could finish, something Pintus would have been quite irritated about had it happened just a month ago.

"We're getting there," said the interrupting, white-coated man. "He's in the next room."

Pintus nodded. He could hardly stand not seeing Cleven for a second longer. They meandered between tables with cages stacked atop them (Pintus swore he saw a monkey chattering away in one of them), and wound their way up to the next set of double doors. Pintus dug his thumb deeper into his palm.

They opened the doors. Mr. Cane sniffed. "I see this is the bird area," he grumbled.

"Indeed 'tis, but only the nocturnal birds," corrected a different white-coated woman who spoke with a thick unidentifiable accent. "If we were to put pahrots and barr-ed owls in the same room, den all ov the pahrots would keep the barr-ed owls up when they were supposed to be sleeping."

If Mr. Cane had looked disapproving and disgusted when the first woman was speaking, then now he looked as though someone was holding dung beneath his pointed nose. Pintus thought he heard him muttering something about disrespectful accents under his breath, and Pintus chuckled before looking around for Cleven. "Which cage?"

"Over there," said the first woman, straightening her glasses. "Head on over."

Pintus hustled to the cage she was indicating and looked in. It was one of the bigger glass cages, and though Pintus suspected that if it had not been his owl, it wouldn't have received such treatment, he was glad to see that Cleven had comfortable living space. He laid the back of his hand against the glass and made a soft cooing noise.

Immediately a small, bandaged saw-whet owl popped its head out from behind a little artificial tree in the cage.

Cleven. Pintus's heart gave a little thrum. He gazed at Cleven for a second, and then made the noise again. Cleven hobbled over and looked at Pintus through the glass, black pupils slowly expanding.

"We had trouble with this one," Pintus heard them saying as he stroked the glass and Cleven pressed his feathers up against it on the other side. "It wasn't wanting to sleep at the correct time for his species. He seemed to be on the same sleeping patterns as humans."

"We trained him," Pintus told her, and then added, "Please, may I take him out?"

"Of course you may, Your Highness," snapped Mr. Cane. "Princes don't need to ask permission."

"Actually, there are many occasions in which a prince may need to ask permission," said Pintus in a calm voice. "And this is one of them." He looked towards the white-coated people. The woman with the glasses said, looking slightly surprised, "Allow me to remove him for you." She hurried over, and lifted the cage top away. She reached her hand down into the cage, but Cleven, with a squeak of panic, darted away from her gloved hand and scuttled over to hide behind a miniscule log.

"Here," said Pintus, leaning over the cage on his tiptoes with his arm outstretched, "let me try." The woman looked at him distrustfully, as though not wanting him to try to retrieve him, so Pintus added, "Trust me."

The woman withdrew her hand hesitantly. "Go on. But . . . *do* be careful as you lift him out."

Pintus carefully and slowly lowered his familiar hand down into the cage, eyes on the log behind which Cleven was hiding. There was a moment where nothing happened, and the woman was about to lean over and ask Pintus to lift away his hand, when Cleven slid his head slowly past the log to look, ready to spring backwards if necessary, at the unexpected arm that was resting in his cage. Pintus curved his lips into an oval shape, and made the familiar cooing sound. As though reassured that it was indeed his old friend, Cleven immediately hopped out from behind the log.

Pintus silently admired Cleven's careful steps and large, trusting eyes. The markings along his feathers, the edges fringed with gold, the careful downward curve of his beak, and the silent, smooth way he walked had always fascinated Pintus, but never so much as now.

Cleven slowly stepped onto Pintus's hand. Pintus felt a rush of love and relief gush over him as soon as his tiny tentative claws touched his hand once more. The familiarity was so wonderful that Pintus let out a whoosh of air and felt like bursting out hugging Cleven – an impulse he had never before experienced – and jumping up and down and laughing wildly in pure joy.

He took Cleven in both of his hands, feeling the soft fragileness of his feathers, and smiled, keeping his composure. "Thank you very much for nursing Cleven back to health. What exactly was wrong with him?"

"Lots of cuts, some dangerously deep. He had needed stitches in one place, although the rest of his injuries just needed time. One leg was sprained."

"I am so grateful," said Pintus. "Now, if you don't mind, I must be excused. I am late for a meeting." He had been hoping that they would have some kind of idea who hurt Cleven and why, but they must not have known any more than the rest of the castle. He didn't know why he had been expecting her to know – after all, the best information he could find on this point was "We found him alone in the streets, lying there dying. We don't know anything else."

"Oh, yes, yes of course, we wouldn't want you to be late. And Your Highness," added the woman in glasses as he turned to leave, "do be extra careful with Cleven. Please do not allow him out of your sight for at least until we know this whole thing has cleared up. The entire event has rather frightened us all."

"Yes, of course," nodded Pintus. He reached up and brushed his fingers against Cleven. It felt as though the little hole missing inside of him which had been there since Cleven had gone missing was now perfectly filled with just the simple weight on his right shoulder. He started for the door again, and opened it.

Mr. Cane raced after him, his shoes making loud clomping noises like a horse's hooves. He hissed, "Let go of that door at once!"

"Why?" asked Pintus.

"Princes have their doors opened for them when they have the option. Always! Do you understand, Prince? *Do you understand?*" he blustered. His glasses were lopsided and his formal face was flushed slightly, as though chastising a naughty child.

"I – I –" Pintus released the door, and it clattered shut. At once Mr. Cane calmed and regained his posture. "I apologize, Your Highness," he murmured to him as the white-coated people immediately scurried over. One of them grasped the handle and pulled open the door.

"Thank you for coming," said the man holding the door, and though Pintus thought it seemed slightly strange for *them* to be thanking *him,* he just smiled and said, "Thank you for having me."

As they hurried out to the hallway, Mr. Cane said, "You are having a meeting today?"

"Oh, yes," Pintus answered.

"And I wasn't invited!" huffed Mr. Cane. "I do wonder what they talk of at those council meetings when I am not present."

Pintus pressed his lips together. It wasn't a council meeting at all. But it *was* a meeting. And Isabella was waiting.

Meeting

Concealed by his cloak and with a newspaper tucked under his arm, Prince Pintus stood at the Coffee Shoppe counter, this time sliding two coins across the counter.

"Both with extra cream and sugar," he told the worker.

After collecting the coffees, he searched around the room until he saw the black-haired, dirty-faced girl vigorously motioning him over. Pintus walked over, every once in a while softly cooing so he could hear Cleven's reply and be assured that he was still there. He sat down across from Isabella, and set down the coffees.

"I see you're thirsty today," Isabella said.

Pintus shook his head. "No, no. This one's for you." He slid it across the table, but Isabella leaned back in her chair and pushed it away.

"I don't take charity."

Pintus stared at her for a moment, then got a grip on himself and said, "It's not charity, Isabella. It's a present, from me to you to thank you for sharing your home with me yesterday."

"Don't make it sound so corny," complained Isabella.

"If I stop, will you take the coffee?" asked Pintus, grinning.

Isabella grinned back. "Absolutely."

She picked up the coffee and brought it up to her lips. "*Ow!*" She waggled her burnt tongue between her lips, eyes crossed. She sloshed the coffee around in the mug. "Are you trying to kill me or what?"

Pintus was laughing. "Can't you see the steam? It's hot. You have to do it like this." He took a dainty sip from his mug, carefully and in a small portion so it wouldn't scald his mouth. Isabella eyed him suspiciously, and mirrored his movements. "Oh." She swallowed it easily and quickly changed the subject. "So, the reason we met here. First of all, why didn't you have Cleven when you met my mom?"

Pintus quickly spilled out the whole story, with the drawbridge and the crocodiles and cranking and the newspaper article. "I have it right here," he said, and withdrew the article from beneath his arm.

Isabella quickly skimmed over it. "Hmm. And this is you they're talking about?" she teased.

"Yes. I . . . I suspect that someone is plotting against me, and against the kingdom."

Isabella sloshed her coffee around in the cup for a second, eyes thoughtful. "I think that much is obvious now, especially that part where you heard hissing voices rasping about disappointing their master. *That* part really creeps me out a bit."

"'Creeps you out?'" repeated Pintus blankly. "What's that supposed to mean?"

"It's commoner slang for 'makes me pretty anxious,'" said Isabella irritably. "But the point is that someone out there is making threats and rebelling against the kingdom, and we – er – *you* need to get to the bottom of it."

Pintus silently nodded. "I can't do it alone."

"Good, because I wasn't planning on not helping," Isabella grinned. Despite her words, though, Pintus noticed she looked relieved to be included.

Suddenly anxious to change the subject, Pintus reached into his cloak and took out Cleven to show Isabella. Cleven stepped nimbly onto the table and surveyed Isabella with his large eyes. Isabella leaned forward to get a better look at the owl, and reached out a hand. Pintus immediately intervened. "He doesn't let strangers hold him," he said. "You needn't try to . . ." he stopped. Cleven had hopped right into Isabella's hand. "What on earth?"

Isabella was smiling perhaps a little smugly as she petted his owl and Cleven closed his eyes in enjoyment. If he were a cat, he'd be purring.

"I . . . I don't know what to say," Pintus stuttered. "He doesn't even like it much when my father holds him, and of course he despises it when Mr. Cane tries to hold him. I don't know why he's . . ." He searched for reasons for why Cleven would so quickly take to trusting Isabella, and couldn't help but notice strange similarities between *himself* and Isabella. They both had the same brown-black eyes, pale skin and nimble fingers, although Isabella's were caked with dirt. Besides their completely different backgrounds, they had quite a lot in common; Pintus had to admit it as he surveyed Isabella further.

Her hair was a different color, black – or was it just the grime from living in her conditions? Cleven nuzzled gently against her hands.

Suddenly a booming crashing noise shook the coffee shop as the door swung open and smashed against the wall, sending cracks spinning up the wall like a spider web.

"Oy!" hollered the man working at the coffee table in protest.

Pintus turned around in his chair. Isabella's knuckles whitened.

A towering, dangerous man was standing impressively in the doorframe. Snow gusted through the door around him. Pintus felt a surge of forbidding shoot through him.

"The king is dead!"

The entire Coffee Shoppe went silent. Pintus felt the room blur around him.

"The king is dead, and the prince missing!"

Isabella dove across the table, knocking the coffees to the ground, and grabbed Pintus by his cloak collar before wrenching him down underneath the table. Pintus's legs flailed out and he opened his mouth to yell but Isabella clapped a hand over his mouth before the sound had formed.

"This coffee shop is being *closed!*" roared the man. "*So get out!*"

Pintus, crouching under the table, thought he heard sobbing from the first people being shoved out the door. Everyone else filed out. Pintus felt cold all over. He watched as the coffee Isabella had knocked to the ground seeped out from the container.

They waited in silence until they heard the door being snapped closed and boards being laid roughly against it. Pintus began to shake.

"Get up, quick!" said Isabella, scrambling out from beneath the table.

Pintus numbly clawed out from under the table. His eyes were wide and haunted. "He wasn't – he *couldn't* be serious, could he?"

"Come this way, we've got to get outta here!" Isabella grasped his elbow and pulled him towards the back of the shop. "Leave it!" she added as he looked back to the newspaper article on the ground and the coffee dribbling on the floor.

"Where's Cleven?" Pintus blared as Isabella gave the wall three almighty kicks. The wall groaned and she kicked it again.

"No worries, I've got 'im!" she gasped. "Mom should be coming immediately; I've given the kick-signal."

Pintus held his head in his hands. "I don't understand!"

"This is what we've been expecting," moaned Isabella. "C'mon, Mom, *c'mon!*"

"Isabella?" the voice came muffled but clear from behind the wall. "Are you there?"

"Mom!" yelped Isabella. "You've gotta get us outta here, someone came to the Shoppe and yelled that the king was dead and the prince missing and we hid under the table so Pintus wouldn't be found and now we're trapped in here!"

"The king is dead?" cried the voice.

"Yes, now help us!"

"All right, back up."

Isabella pulled Pintus backwards. He tripped over his own feet. There was a banging noise and then something heavy pounded against the other side of the wall. The wall leaned in towards them.

"Again!" cried Isabella.

There was a series of footsteps and then the something smacked against the wall again and it gave way. With a crashing noise splinters of painted wood went flying in every direction and a dusty figure dashed forward.

Mrs. Carole ran with her arms outstretched to Isabella and the dazed Pintus. "Are you two all right?"

"We're fine now, but I doubt that it's going to last," said Isabella grimly.

Pintus tried to get a grip on himself and the entire situation seemed to play out before his eyes. "I need to get back to the castle!"

Isabella gaped at him. "Have you gone mad? You need to stay here so we can figure this out!"

"No! If Father is dead, I need to be there, for my kingdom!" Pintus ran his fingers through his hair. "I need to go see the front guard. He was expecting this."

"I – If you're going, I'm coming too," said Isabella.

"You can't – you aren't part of the castle," Pintus reminded her.

Isabella gave him a cold, hard stare and said in a deadly calm voice, "I'm coming."

Pintus looked into her determined eyes and after a long moment of silence, gave one small tight nod.

Mrs. Carole laid a hand on his shoulder. "Good luck." She wiped a tear that was slipping down her bony cheek and said in a choked voice, "I. . . I am so very sorry for the loss of your father. More than . . . than you could ev-ver guess."

Pintus looked at her, pressing his lips together to keep them from trembling. "Thank you, Mrs. Carole," he whispered. "Thank you."

Narrow Escape

Cleven bouncing on Pintus's shoulder, the two very different twelve-year-olds ran down the cobblestone street glazed with ice. It was an entirely different world now. Every shop was tight closed and with boards slammed against them reading CLOSED in unarguable red letters. The fruit stand was sprawled on the ground, fruit scattered in every direction, and there wasn't a snowball-throwing soul to be seen. The castle loomed out in the distance, framed by the misty clouds.

"This way," said Pintus lowly as they neared the castle. He crouched as they approached the moat and whispered, "You stay here where you can see and hear and I'll go up to the front guard."

Isabella began to open her mouth to argue, but quickly shut it. "Okay."

"Take Cleven," Pintus requested.

Isabella reached out and Cleven slipped into her hands.

"I'll be back as soon as possible." Without waiting for a response from Isabella, Pintus carefully made his way towards the moat at a low crawl. Ready to leap to his feet and scramble away if necessary, Pintus gave eight shrill whistles and waited. He could see the front guard on the other side of the moat. His head snapped up attentively and he peered around with wide eyes.

There was a moment of tense silence in which Pintus clutched the grass and tried to hold his breath, and then slowly and hesitantly, the front guard lowered the bridge a fraction of an inch. Pintus curved his lips into a small circle again and whistled eight more times to encourage him.

The front guard let down the bridge the rest of the way, and Pintus jumped to his feet. He pulled the cloak over his eyes and ran across. It seemed to take much longer to go across the bridge than usual, and Pintus could hear his heart throbbing and pounding. The front guard was waiting for him at the end of the bridge next to the crank.

"Front guard!" gasped Pintus. "Thank goodness you're all right. Did you hear? The king is supposedly dead, and they think me to be missing!"

He looked anxiously into the front guard's face, but he saw no flicker of emotion. Pintus had expected a much larger reaction. "Er. . .front guard?"

"I have to warn you," growled the front guard. "You must leave. You are no longer in power here. Now, get out! Get *out!*" He took a big step forward and Pintus stumbled backwards. But he held his ground.

"No, front guard, I won't! Listen here, I need your help. You suspected something was going to happen, something like this, and now –"

"Didn't you hear me? *Intruder, get out!*"

"And didn't *you hear me?* I said *no!* What are you talking about! I deserve more respect than this, front guard! How dare you call me an intruder? Now listen to me, we are faced with a serious problem here!" Pintus was enraged at the way the front guard was speaking to him. No one at the castle was ever to speak to him like that. *Intruder* – how dare he call him. . . . What was the meaning of this?

The front guard shifted uncomfortably. "*Listen to me. There is a new heir now. You have no power over me –* you are no more to me than a common street boy."

"I'm your *friend*," pointed out Pintus. "And if I mean no more than a street boy to you now, then why did you lower the drawbridge for me?"

"Listen, boy," growled the front guard, his eyes becoming a little less hard and cold for a moment, reverting almost to the point of looking like the old front guard. "Things have changed. The king is gone now, and there's a new heir. It's too late for this. You've . . . you've got to leave, go into hiding. She's after you, Pintus."

"Why? Why me?"

"Because you're the king's son, and she hasn't found the king's will yet. She is assuming that the kingdom was supposed to be left to you after the king's death."

"What d'you mean 'she'? The heir isn't – it isn't a woman, is it? How on earth did –" He had to stop and remind himself what was important. "How can she have not found the will yet?"

"I've said too much already. All I can say is you've got to get out of here, and immediately."

Pintus stared at him in dismay. "You can't just –"

"I'm losing my temper," said the front guard, eyes becoming hard again. "I am going to turn around and when I turn back again, you had better be gone or else I'm calling out more guards to get you out of here."

"But front guard, I need your help! When will they announce Father's will?"

The front guard turned swiftly around. Pintus moaned, and slapped his hand against his forehead in frustration. He thought to himself that he should run now, get out of there before he turned around again, but thought again that the chances of his friend calling a group of guards to chase him away seemed pretty remote. But was it worth the risk? Yet even as he was battling with his thoughts the guard turned around again. He looked furious.

"I warned you," he said angrily, and opened the door into the castle. He stepped forward into the doorframe and shouted, "*Intruder alert! Intruder alert! More guards, I need more guards! Intruder alert!*"

Pintus whirled around to face the moat again. From across it he could see Isabella leaping up from behind a bush. He saw her mouth moving quickly up and down, but the roar of panic in his ears was too loud for him to make out her words. He heard thundering down the steps behind him and the clanking of armor and without another thought, sprinted towards the drawbridge. His feet struck against the drawbridge as he started to run across. He could hear the new group of guards yelling at him to "hold it right there", and the front guard bellowing to "hurry up and catch him".

"The drawbridge!" one of them cried. "The drawbridge, crank up the drawbridge!"

Pintus was reaching the end of the drawbridge when suddenly it arched sharply upwards. Pintus wobbled to keep his balance. The chains that connected the drawbridge to the castle had been pulled straight by the crank, and he was being hauled backwards. Pintus struggled not to fall the rest of the way down the drawbridge and into their fingertips. His fingers scrabbled desperately at the smooth wood and began to slip.

"No!" groaned Pintus, and rolled his feet to the side of the drawbridge to keep himself from sliding the rest of the way down. The crocodiles were swimming directly beneath Pintus, eyes hungry and staring straight at him. It looked like doom either way.

"Pintus!" shouted a voice, and there was a thumping noise on the opposite side of the drawbridge, on the side closest to the water. Pintus looked up. A pale hand was clenched on the end of the drawbridge.

"Isabella?!" Pintus said in amazement.

"No, it's Lucas the fruit selling man!" Isabella yelled, and strongly pulled herself up onto the drawbridge. Pintus reached out his hand desperately and she grabbed it at once, pulling him easily up next to her. Pintus almost laughed at himself for automatically thinking, *pretty strong, for a girl.*

They were almost completely drawn back to the castle. Pintus took a chance and glanced backwards. The guards were frozen in place, staring in bafflement at Isabella. One of them raised a shaking finger. "Is . . . is that . . .?"

Another said with eyes as large as Cleven's, "But . . . how did Pintus find out?"

"It doesn't matter, you fools!" exclaimed another guard, trying to look brave though Pintus noticed he looked rather confused as well. "Keep cranking!"

"Quick!" said Isabella, lunging for Pintus's hand. "We're jumping!"

"*What?*" yelped Pintus. "I've had enough of jumping into moats, thank you very much!"

"Come on, we've got to, before they come back to their senses!" cried Isabella, and without further ado, leapt straight off the drawbridge, dragging Pintus down with her.

Splash.

Sploosh.

First Isabella hit the water, and then Pintus followed. He struggled quickly to the surface, thoughts full of angry crocodiles and razor-sharp teeth. "Go! Go!" Pintus shouted to Isabella, who had just popped her head out of the water. "The crocodiles! Head to the other side – go!"

The drawbridge clanged down again, inches above their heads. Isabella yelled out and immediately started vigorously swimming towards the other side of the moat.

Sprays of water that she kicked up splashed in Pintus's face, but he hardly noticed. *Just keep swimming, just keep swimming.*

Isabella shrieked and recoiled.

"What? What's the matter?" Pintus demanded.

"I felt something rough brush up against my legs!"

"Just keep going!"

"I – I –" Isabella started forward again, though seeming slightly more hesitant. But her eyes took on their usual hard braveness almost immediately. "We're almost there," she called to Pintus.

"Yes, yes, so keep going," Pintus encouraged, flinching as he felt water stir beneath him slightly, as though something was moving around him.

Isabella finally reached the end of the moat and desperately stretched her body upwards. "I can't reach it!"

"I can, I'll get up and pull you up!"

He swam forward and dug his fingers into the earth. His arms weren't nearly as strong as Isabella's, but he was taller. He pulled up and scrambled out onto the ground. Violent shivers immediately caused his teeth to clack together.

"Now help me!" pleaded Isabella.

Pintus leaned over and grasped her wrists. Isabella kicked her feet wildly, and he yanked. Isabella was far lighter than he thought she would be, and without almost any effort on Pintus's part, her bony body came soaring through the air and landed beside him. Isabella let out a breath of relief. "We made it!"

"Not yet we didn't," Pintus said grimly, and pointed. The guards were all swarming to the drawbridge that had been let down again.

Isabella scrambled to her feet. "Well, we'd better go then! Come on!" She started running away from the castle. Pintus's chest hurt and his feet ached, but he sprang to his feet. He shook his sopping hair out of his face and raced after her. Behind him he could hear the guards howling and shoving at each other as they crossed the bridge, armor making such a loud racket that nearby nesting birds took flight.

Wait – birds? *Birds!*

"Isabella!" cried Pintus from behind her. "Where's Cleven?"

"He's coming!" hollered back Isabella. "Look behind you! Now save your breath!"

Pintus twisted around in mid-run, and saw a streak of golden feathers. Cleven was flying behind them, keeping up the rear. Pintus whirled around again and tried to move his legs faster.

"Quick, Pintus!" Isabella called, and cut into the woods to the side of the path they were scrabbling down. "There's a path leading to the village this way!"

"I've lost sight of them, but they're probably just around the corner!" Pintus panted.

"Perfect then, follow me!"

Will

Pintus opened his eyes. He knew immediately that it had not all been just a terrible nightmare because whatever he was lying on was hard and made his back stiff and uncomfortable. If he were lying in his bed at the castle right now, his many assistants would see to it that his bed was soft and comfortable under all circumstances. He also knew because he felt the crustiness of dirt on his body and the sweat from all the running still against his skin. If he were still in the castle, the servants would have long by now scrubbed it carefully away.

He blinked. He was facing a low grainy wooden ceiling. Definitely not the carefully and smoothly painted cream-colored walls of the castle. The only familiar thing was the softness of Cleven at his wrist. Pintus sat up. Where was he? He peered around in the darkness, and slowly came to recognize his surroundings as Isabella's hideout.

"You're finally up?" asked Isabella's voice from across the room.

Pintus jumped and turned around in the direction of her voice.

"Yes. I . . . I don't quite remember getting here."

"We ran through the woods, managed to get to the back of the abandoned shop, and squirmed through the brick wall to safety just as the guards turned the corner. You keeled over and fell right asleep, but I stayed up a while." She paused. "It was pretty scary, I could hear the guards running around behind the hideout, yelling to each other to look in certain places and not giving up until well past the moon rising."

Pintus strained to remember. He could recall fumbling with the loose bricks to open the secret entrance, trying to be of some assistance, but Isabella impatiently pushing him aside to work faster, and a little of running desperately through the woods. It all seemed like a distant, blurring nightmare.

"So what now?" asked Pintus.

"Well, we've gotta take things one step at a time. Right now, what we've gotta do is somehow listen to the reading of your father's will," said Isabella. "I have a feeling something important is going to happen there."

There was a slight pause, and then Pintus said quietly, "I wonder how it happened."

"What?"

"My. . .my father. How did he die? The servants, and the guards. . .they should have been able to – to protect him." He tried to control his voice, but the last words came out as a croak and his lips were trembling. He felt immensely grateful that it was dim and Isabella couldn't see him.

"I don't know." Pintus jumped. Isabella's voice had suddenly gotten a lot closer, right next to him. Her voice was soft and gentle, very different from her usual hard, determined voice. She could have been talking to a kitten. "I don't know."

He wanted to stop talking, stop opening his wounds further, but he couldn't. "I still can't quite believe it." His voice cracked at the end, and he looked away. He didn't want to see the sympathy in Isabella's eyes or hear the sadness in her voice. He just wanted to. . .what *did* he want to do?

Isabella took his hand and gave it a squeeze. That was all he needed. He straightened himself and took a deep breath.

"How do we find out when the will's reading will be?" he asked.

"We have to start somewhere," sighed Isabella. "Let's go check out the village.

"But the guards are searching for us," pointed out Pintus. "Couldn't they capture us and –"

"Why would they bother? I mean, they're probably at the castle as we speak, trying to find that will."

Pintus nodded, but his attention was suddenly caught by a glint of gold at the other side of the small cramped room. He stood up slowly, craning his neck to get a better look at it. Then, more out of curiosity than anything else, he wandered over in that direction and found himself looking down at one of the cardboard boxes that Isabella and her mother sat on. "Here, pass me a candle," said Pintus suddenly.

He heard Isabella rummaging about for a moment, and then the striking noise of a match being lit. She didn't question him, sensing that it wasn't a good time. She handed him the lit candle. Pintus took it and leaned over, looking down at the bottom of the cardboard box. Something thin and golden was trailing out from beneath the cardboard box. Pintus reached down with his free hand and carefully curled his finger underneath it and pulled up.

The box leaned backwards a little bit and the rest of the thin gold something slipped out. It was a tiny golden chain connecting to a small circular locket. Isabella leaned over to look. Pintus clicked open the locket with his fingernail, and peered inside. There was a dusty, though carefully drawn, picture of a bearded man with twinkling eyes and a lively smile on his face. "That's odd," murmured Pintus. "That looks a little bit like –" He stopped.

Isabella elbowed him. "Like *what?*"

"Like my father," whispered Pintus, wondering if he was just thinking too much about King Horace and was seeing things. But as he squinted at it in the flickering light of the flame, there was no denying the carefully trimmed beard and familiar face. On the other side of the locket, a tiny folded up piece of parchment stuck out. Pintus pulled it out immediately and, with an increasing feeling of unease, recognized his father's scrolling handwriting.

I see your lovely face and

My heart stands still,

Filled with your grace and

All goodwill.

Live for the moment

Consequence unheeding.

Love, be mine, all else unneeding.

Pintus looked up. Isabella licked her lips. "We ought to hang on to that," she muttered. "Stick it back in the locket."

Pintus obeyed, and stuffed the chained necklace into his cloak pocket. As he reached in, he felt his fingers touch something papery and suddenly remembered the fortune cookies. With some indifference and a pang of disbelief he realized that it was only a few days ago that he had gone with the front guard to examine fortunes at the *Enutrof Seikooc.*

Isabella looked slightly unnerved at what they had just seen and read. Shaking her head, she said, "Let's focus on that later. Now, we need to go to the village and find out about that will."

At the town square a crowd had gathered up and around a messenger from the castle who was shouting news over the roar of the icy wind. Isabella and Pintus elbowed their way up to the front of the crowd and listened with attentive ears.

"Hear 'e, hear 'e!" cried the messenger. "The crowning ceremony of the new heir is *today!* Today at the front of the castle! Hear 'e, hear 'e, today at the front of the castle as soon as the sun has reached the middle of the sky! Hear 'e, hear 'e!"

Pintus looked at Isabella. "Today?" he said in astonishment. Usually the next heir waited at least four days out of respect for the last ruler before the crowning. Instead the new leader was hosting the crowning ceremony on the day after the King's death. Rage boiled inside of Pintus at the disrespect shown, but he also felt slightly relieved that they at least wouldn't have to wait in suspense for four days.

"As soon as the sun has reached the middle of the sky, today," said Isabella in a stunned voice. "I can't believe this. We *need* to be there."

"Of course we need to be there," said Pintus stressfully. He automatically reached up to lightly touch Cleven beneath his cloak to reassure himself. The soft cooing of his owl calmed him. "But the sun is just now beginning to light the kingdom. We have some time."

"Time? *Time?* Have you gone mad? We don't have any time at all!" Isabella squeezed her eyes shut and took a deep breath. "We have to head towards the castle. The sun will be in the middle of the sky in a matter of hours."

Pintus felt like screaming out in despair at the thought of going back to the castle again after his so recent experience, but held himself together. He nodded swiftly, biting his lip to keep himself from letting out any tears. *Don't be a baby,* he thought sternly, but the pain was fresh inside of him and he couldn't not "be a baby" with ease. He took a shaky breath and nodded once more. "Let's go."

So without further ado, they took off on their exhausted legs in the direction of the castle.

A large ceremonial stand had been set up with golden drapes slung decoratively over the top and a long fancy carpet rolling down a couple small dainty steps. On the center of the stage stood a polished table with curved legs displaying lavishly designed carvings. Atop the fancy table was a smooth wooden box fastened shut with a tight elegant lock. Everyone knew with a buzzing excitement that the crown was kept in there. The snow had subsided now, and though the air was crisp and cold, it was perfect weather for a crowning. A crowd of peasants was gathered around the stand, all of them looking eager to see the action. It seemed to take years for an announcer to finally step to the edge of the stage and speak. He was wearing a luxurious red uniform.

"Welcome to the Crowning Ceremony. Before we begin, let us all bow our heads for a moment of silence to honor the Ki–" There was a sharp impatient sounding cry from behind the stand, and the announcer stumbled to a stop.

"Er. . ." he skipped quickly on, as though he had never begun that sentence. Pintus clamped his hands into fists.

"Our new ruler," he introduced in a rich flowing voice, "Queen Lamia!"

And out she stepped. She was a tall, majestic woman wearing queenly clothing and walking in a prideful way. There was something cold about the way she looked at the crowd, something false about her would-be charming smile that was more like a leer. Her expensive clothing trailed on the floor behind her. She raised one hand rather lazily and curtsied.

The announcer backed up and withdrew a long, faded, yellow scroll. He opened it and let the bottom trail on the floor. "The king's will," the announcer said, raising the scroll in indication. "It reads, '*I leave my kingdom with care and love to the kind hearted Lamia, who shall rule the kingdom with wisdom and –*'"

"No!" A voice shattered through the crowd from the side of the stand. Pintus whirled around to look as did the rest of the crowd. The announcer stammered to a stop. Queen Lamia started hissing at him with an enraged look on her face, but he had frozen to listen to the voice.

"No!" it shouted again, and the voice sounded distantly familiar to Pintus, though different somehow, crazed and desperate when he almost always heard it calm. "Lies, they speak *lies!* That is not the will!" Suddenly a man with thin rectangular glasses and a familiar face leapt onto the stage.

Mr. Cane!

Pintus had difficulty not shouting out in surprise. Isabella looked frozen in place, petrified by what was happening on the stage.

Mr. Cane brandished an even yellower and, no doubt, even longer scroll tied up carefully in a thick cylinder above his head. "This is the real will!" he cried. "They are speaking *lies!*" He stopped in his rant for a second, and his eyes widened. *"Pintus, catch!"*

He thrust the will into the air.

Realization

Pintus saw the will flying through the air, but he couldn't believe it. That was the one thing that could possibly save him and Isabella, and a hundred bystanders could snatch it away before he could. It seemed to soar through the air in slow motion as Pintus leaped backwards to catch it before it sailed out of his reach. He saw Isabella's mouth moving, felt Cleven dart off his shoulder at his sudden movement, and distantly heard the new heir screaming in fury for them to seize Mr. Cane, but none of it mattered – he just had to close his fingers around that will.

"Umph!" Pintus crashed to the ground, and the will thumped lightly on top of him. Everything came sharply back into focus. Isabella was at his side as soon as she could get back through the crowd. Her dark sharp eyes scanned over his face. Pintus looked towards the stage and saw Mr. Cane being dragged away. He could hardly believe that the calm, irritating Mr. Cane had just done that.

"Seize them! *Seize them!*" shrieked Queen Lamia. She was pointing her ringed fingers down at the crowd now, threatening every one of them with their lives. Isabella yanked Pintus to his feet. He quickly scrambled to pick up the will. "Run for it!"

By the time they were halfway back to the village, the guards had only just arranged themselves in an organized enough fashion to chase after them. Pintus felt strange – light-headed and dizzy. Disbelieving. Confused. *Exhausted.* He had never run this much in two days in his life. At the same time, though, a new energy seemed to be flooding through him. Excitement and fear and euphoria thundered through his veins as he escaped the horrific scene.

"Quick, back to the Coffee Shoppe!"

Pintus felt immensely thankful that there was no snow falling right now as he followed Isabella to the abandoned building. She struggled with the boards covering the brick wall at the back of the Coffee Shoppe for a moment. "You know what? Scratch that. Let's go to the hideout. Maybe's Mom's there – though lots of the time she's out."

"Where is she when she's out?" asked Pintus. Isabella shrugged as she crept along the backs of the different shops.

She stopped behind the building housing her mother's hideaway. "I dunno for sure," she admitted, feeling around the bricks. Pintus found this rather strange, maybe even a bit alarming, but then realized most of the time he never knew where his father was, seeing as how being the king he was always so busy, and it was probably the same with Isabella.

Isabella popped out a brick, loosening the others to make the passage. It hit the ground, sending a puff of frost into the air. Pintus found himself staring at it.

Isabella nudged him. "It's open." She slipped through the narrow space, and Pintus followed, the will tight in his grip. Cleven flew skillfully after them and landed comfortably on Pintus's shoulder, back where he belonged. They worked quickly to close up the hole in the wall, and then Isabella lit some candles.

They stared at each other for a moment, each of their faces barely visible by the low flickering of the candles. Then, when he could stand it no longer, Pintus burst out,

"*We've got it!*" He held the will high in the air. "We've got the will!"

"We did it!" squeaked Isabella. Her eyes were shining in excitement. "We really did it." She took a deep breath, a wide and rare smile on her face. "So now what?"

"We read it," said Pintus, and they hurried out of the hallway and into the room. They both sat down on the cardboard boxes, and Pintus unrolled the crisply furled parchment with quivering fingers.

In the Name of the Law . . .

I, King Ericson Horace Sacco, hereby leave my Kingdom in the hands of my one true love: Carole Sanderson. In the event of an unfortunate early death, my son Pintus Sacco shall be put under her care. My message to her: Though we are now more separate than if we were across the planet from one another, my love for you has not wavered, and never shall as long as I live. Or die.

Witnesses

Gesto Relient

Harrison Cane

Pintus looked at Isabella, eyes wide. "He left his kingdom and everything else to some secret love," he said in astonishment. He tried not to feel too much betrayal. "But. . . I thought after Mother died he never fell in love again. He told me himself." Cleven nipped at Pintus's ear comfortingly.

Isabella said suddenly, "Carole Sanderson?" Her face was very white.

"Yes, look here." His fingers fluttered with the will. They were trembling too much to hold steady.

Isabella peered over. "Impossible," she whispered, but Pintus only half heard her. He was reaching into his grimy cloak pocket. He wiggled his fingers around in the sea of fortune cookies, searching for the locket attached to the golden chain. He hooked his finger around it, and then pulled it out. "The poem," he said in a whispery voice. "I think – I think that it's from my father, and he's writing it to this mystery love of his. But . . . why was it in your safe place?"

Isabella drew in a quick sharp breath of air. "Pintus..."

"I just don't understand how it is that he even had a mystery love – I'm pretty sure Mother was the only one." A rush of pain swept over him at the thought of his father so quickly replacing the mother he had hardly known. "And what does it mean when it says 'Though we are now more separate than if we were across the planet from one another'? Do you think the castle didn't approve of his marrying her? Maybe they wouldn't let them marry, so that's why. . ."

"Pintus –" Isabella looked dazed and a little frightened.

"I'm supposed to be under her care, but how do we even find her? I'm positive that Queen Lamia is *not* Carole Sanderson. I just don't see how –"

"*Pintus!*" exploded Isabella. "Listen! My *mom's name is Carole Sanderson!*"

Pintus stared at her. He suddenly felt very cold. "What – what do you mean?"

"I mean that *I'm* Isabella Sanderson, *Mom's* Carole Sanderson! *Sanderson!* I'm missing my dad, and you don't have a mom, and in your father's will it says that he's left his kingdom to his one true love, Carole Sanderson! Then there is the love poem with a drawing of your dad in it. . ."

Pintus jumped to his feet, his head spinning and the world swirling around him. "The family tree book," he said in amazement. "Isabella, I had a family tree I was supposed to be copying, and there was this big blank spot on my Mother's side!" He looked at her eyes that mirrored his own, and, with excitement and terror surging through him, thought about how Cleven had so quickly taken to her when they first met and how Mrs. Carole had looked so strikingly familiar to Pintus when he first met her. "Isabella. . ."Pintus struggled to make his possibility sound less crazy than even he thought it was. "I think . . . is it possible . . . she is my *mother?* Are-are we *siblings?*"

Isabella leaped to her feet, the scrolled will in her hands. She looked petrified. "We need to go find Mom and talk to her, *now.*" She ran for the hallway, candle jiggling in her hand.

Pintus jogged after her. "I thought you said you had no idea where she was," he called.

"I never said I had no idea," called back Isabella, "I just said I didn't know for sure."

Pintus hastily caught up with her. "Where do you *guess* she is, then?"

"I'm thinking that she went out to the creek to get a new supply of water," answered Isabella, sliding out the brick. A beam of light from the small rectangular hole shone in and made a golden highlight on Isabella's face. She blew out her candle. "There's a creek along a path through the woods," she said, continuing to unravel the entrance way. "The creek is a common place where people like us meet when we need to get fresh and clean – uh – clean-*ish* water."

"Oh. Right. Okay, well, you lead the way, then," said Pintus, as though it might have been possible for him to lead the way to a place he had never before known existed. Pintus thought that if they were under regular circumstances Isabella would have said something snappy or sarcastic, but she was silent this time as she took away the last brick.

"C'mon."

Witch

Pintus had never been in these woods before, except for the time he and Isabella had cut through them to get to the hideout. But that had been only a short distance; this time they would have to hike to almost the very center, the very *heart*, of the woods to make it to the creek, and they had to do it fast. Pintus felt desperately clumsy constantly stepping into thick, seeping mud, brambles snaring into his soiled cloak.

He jumped at every small noise, thinking of slithering snakes and monstrous bears, but it was always nothing more than a nimble bird or a skittering squirrel. Pintus silently envied both how smoothly and silently Isabella crept through the woods like an animal herself. He also admired her cool calm attitude whenever some sort of noise caused Pintus to let out a little squeak of terror.

The woods seemed to stretch on and on forever. Cold, dusty snow covered everything. It seemed as if it took all the snow and ice in the woods ten times longer than the rest of the kingdom to thaw out. The only comfort was that the trees around them were a bit of protection from the raving winds that were screaming rebellion above them. The trees waved back and forth, the branches trembled, and though the snow had still not started up again, it was desperately cold. Pintus felt sorry for Isabella, who was wearing nothing but thin rags. Cleven was fluttering and quivering on his shoulder, incapable of staying still for more than a couple seconds. "Are we almost there?" asked Pintus, gritting his teeth to stop them from chattering.

"Nearly," murmured Isabella. "*Hold it!*"

"Get down, quick!" she hissed, throwing herself down against the frozen ground. Pintus flung himself down next to her, heart thumping in his chest. They were silent, listening for several moments. In the distance they could hear harsh voices calling to one another.

"We'd better hurry." Isabella looked grimly scared. "I think something wrong."

Of course there's something wrong, Pintus thought frantically. He avoided Isabella's gaze and hoped she didn't see that tears of frustration were whelming up in his eyes. *Everything's wrong.*

Suddenly Isabella jumped to her feet and set off at a run. Snow kicked up behind her feet. Pintus ran after her, breathing deeply, trying to chase out the desperate emotion that had taken control of him. He blinked rapidly and kept running. He soon caught up with Isabella, and together they crept through the woods in direction of the creek.

When they finally reached it, Pintus sensed immediately that others had come before them. No, he didn't sense it – he *knew* it. He could tell from the clanging of armor and the rough voices of soldiers. Were *the castle guards still after them?*

Pintus ducked behind a tree and watched, heart pounding so loudly in his ears he was sure that his enemies could hear it.

Surrounding the thin, half-frozen creek was a group of armored men. Swords gleamed at their sides. Most noticeably of all, though, was Queen Lamia. She stood impressively in front of her minions and faced across the creek. She slowly raised her arm to point across the water at a single bony woman that Pintus immediately recognized, with a pang of dread, as Mrs. Carole.

"You have irked me enough, Sanderson," said Queen Lamia. Pintus could see hatred in her eyes. "I have known your secret for many years now, and not until today have I possessed the power to reveal it. You – are – a – *witch*."

"You're out of your mind!" said Mrs. Carole in fury and disgust. "That's your excuse? What kind of a coward would corner an old enemy alone in the woods with a miniature army?"

Queen Lamia turned to her miniature army. Her eyes flashed in triumph. Her face was so smug it hurt to look at it. Pintus gritted his teeth.

"I declare this woman a witch, and so she is a witch. If anyone objects –" She peered around at the armored men with narrowed eyes, "they are free to part company with their heads."

"This is madness!" cried Mrs. Carole angrily from the other side of the creek. "H-How can you possibly believe –?"

"We must take her to the castle and imprison her at once. She is to be burned at the stake within the week for her crimes of witchcraft."

Queen Lamia lowered her arm from its position pointing into the air, one angular index finger pointed straight across the creek at Mrs. Carole, *"Seize her!"*

Next to Pintus, Isabella lurched forward, arms raised and mouth jutted open in rage. Pintus, wide-eyed and horrified, flung himself forward and snatched her by her shoulders. "Don't!" he exclaimed. "There's too many of them! We'd never make it out alive."

Isabella struggled fiercely. Pintus could see Mrs. Carole fighting against them, but she was soon engulfed by the sheer number of the vicious knights and went down out of Pintus's sight. Isabella let out a scream of terror and fury, but it wasn't heard over the yells of the knights, screeches of the new heir, and protests of Mrs. Carole.

"No! Shush, shush!" gasped Pintus.

Tears were streaming down Isabella's face and she was still fighting against Pintus to get at them. "Those monsters, those awful beasts!" she moaned.

"Hush Isabella, *quiet!* We've still got some time – they won't kill her today, didn't you hear them? We have until at least tomorrow morning to rescue her."

Isabella slowly calmed. Her breathing was still jagged and hoarse. "You're right. We – we've got to g-go. But we *have* to find out when that monster is going to b-burn her."

"Right," whispered Pintus shakily. Was it *his* mother as well as Isabella's who the Queen's minions were forcing into a cart now that was to wobble off back to the castle? Could it possibly be the mother that for so many years he thought he had lost? He couldn't lose her again. They would have to do something – anything – to get her back and take Queen Lamia out of power. But Isabella was right – they couldn't do anything until they had some kind of time frame, some facts to rely on as they went about figuring when to act and how fast.

Pintus inched forward. The Queen was standing, haughtily watching the actions of her soldiers as they shoved her enemy into the horse-pulled cart.

A knight scurried over to her. "Enemy contained, Your Highness."

"Excellent," said the new heir with a dreadful smile on her face. "She shall be burned at the stake . . . but not immediately. We must give our witchy guest a chance to think about her situation first."

"When shall we dispose of her?" asked the knight.

Queen Lamia pondered for a second. Pintus could almost see the wicked, twisted gears of her mind turning. "Three days," she said at last. She looked with deep satisfaction towards the cart. "Three days to consider her sins."

"Yes, Your Highness."

Pintus eyed the castle that had once been his home with a combination of longing and disgust. Isabella stood rigidly beside of him, not even letting out a whimper as the icy wind gusted into their faces. Even in such a desperate situation, Pintus couldn't help but think: *Pretty tough, for a girl.*

On Pintus's shoulder, Cleven shifted uneasily at the sight of the castle.

"So what's the plan?" said Isabella finally. Pintus looked back, and pressed himself against the red-bricked corner of the coffee house that he had been peering around.

"Isabella, I honestly don't know how we can rescue your mother," said Pintus. "If the new heir thinks she's a witch, there's not much we can do. Remember what she said? *'I declare this woman a witch, and so she is a witch. If anyone objects –'"*

"'' – they are free to part company with their heads', I know. But the thing is, we've got nothing to lose at this point. You've been cast out of the castle, my mother's been captured, and that imposter of a new heir is taking over the kingdom. We have everything to gain, and I say we take our chances to gain it."

Pintus swallowed, and Cleven shifted again. Isabella shoved her dirty black hair out of her face. "We have to do something. This just – isn't – right. It's unjust. And we have to do something about it."

Pintus looked at her. She had the same determined look on her face that she had worn the day the Coffee Shoppe had been shut down and Pintus was telling her she didn't have to come with him. She was determined.

Isabella was determined, and when Isabella was determined, almost nothing could stop her. And this comforted Prince Pintus and his pet saw-whet owl a great deal.

"We have three days," said Pintus. "Three days to come up with a plan, put this mystery together, rescue your mother, and save the kingdom."

Isabella's eyes looked wet and ready to cry, but she held herself together. "We can do it."

Pintus reached over and squeezed her hand. "I know we can."

Advice

Pintus and Isabella both decided that they needed as much time as possible to carefully plan everything out, and though Isabella had been slightly hesitant to rescue her mother later rather than immediately, they had eventually agreed to go in and save her just before the sun rose on the third day.

"The more time we have to figure this out, the better," muttered Pintus.

The first thing they did upon returning from the woods was to sneak into the Coffee Shoppe through the passageway that led to Isabella's hideout. The Coffee Shoppe was exactly as they had left it – Pintus's coffee cup was still lying on the floor, the newspaper still crumpled next to it. They had secretly dragged one light table and two chairs carefully out to the frosty area next to Isabella's hideout. They had strategically placed it so it wasn't visible but they could sit at the table and still have some light. It became their main place to sit and plan. The shock of the entire situation seemed to be wearing off a little for Isabella, though she still seemed rather numb and dazed.

Pintus must have read his father's will a thousand times, and asked himself over and over, *Could it truly be about my mother?* They had spent the rest of the haunted day reading and re-reading the will and trying to hunt down small scraps of parchment that they could piece together and use to have Pintus write down some sort of plan. Isabella couldn't read or write, but she seemed to enjoy watching Pintus carefully draw his letters. Pintus was even lucky enough to find a small smashed bottle of ink on the cobblestone street, and after a minute of coaxing he managed to gain a little sacrifice of Cleven's new winter feathers and used the quill to write on the small scraps paper they had found.

We have to use our time wisely, Pintus thought again and again. *There's no point if we don't plan all of this out perfectly.* He had never wanted something to go as well as this. He could not afford a failure. That was not an option. Mrs. Carole's life was at stake – and not only that but the entire mystery and the hope to regain control of the kingdom was at risk as well.

The cold day darkened into a navy blue sky. The air was cold and crisp. It smelled clean. Fresh.

Isabella pressed her fingers against her forehead. "So much has happened," she whispered, "in one day."

Pintus hesitantly laid a hand on her shoulder. "I know. But we don't have time to dwell on this . . . it's nighttime now and it's starting to frost already. We need to go into the hideout again."

Isabella didn't move, but just sat there with her fingers pressed against her forehead. Pintus nervously withdrew his hand. They sat in silence for a long moment, and then Isabella made one small, barely audible noise. "Why us?"

Her question hung in the air. Pintus didn't need to ask what she was talking about. But he didn't answer – he couldn't think of anything to say.

Pintus didn't know how long they sat there at the table from the Coffee Shoppe in silence. He watched as the moon slowly rose above them, white and glowing above the nearby woods. He wished Isabella would break the silence, or jump up to clear out the passage – even a sarcastic comment would be a big relief on Pintus's side.

They continued sitting there in silence until suddenly from around the abandoned building came the sound of feet, crunching through the snow. Pintus sucked in a deep breath of air, eyes wide. *"Isabella!"* he hissed.

Isabella jolted up and looked at Pintus. "What?"

"Shhh! I think I hear footsteps!" Pintus was petrified. There wasn't enough time to uncover the secret entrance, no chance of being able to blend in underneath the table. Even running didn't sound like much of an option – Pintus was beyond exhausted, mentally and physically. So they tensely sat, bolt upright, waiting in terror as the footsteps came closer and closer. Finally whatever it was rounded the corner, and caught sight of Isabella and Pintus frozen in their seats.

Crunch, crunch, crunch.

The figure neared them and came closer and closer until finally –

It reached up and pulled down the hood. Pintus realized with an increasing feeling of panic that it was the front guard. But it didn't look like the front guard – a secretive black cloak was drawn over him and he wasn't wearing his uptight uniform.

"Your Highness!" blurted out the front guard, and rushed forward.

Pintus banged against the end of his chair, eyes wide and panicked. His hand swung out as he scrambled to get up and accidentally smacked it hard into Isabella's gut.

"Ouch!"

"We need to get out of here!" Pintus yelped.

"No! No! No, do not fear," begged the front guard.

Pintus noticed Isabella attempting to make herself as unnoticeable as possible. Pintus marveled for a second how the Isabella he had first met would never have tried not to be noticed, and then quickly flashed back to the present. He looked at the front guard with a mixture of fear and anger.

"What are you doing here, traitor?" asked Pintus.

"Traitor?" said the front guard incredulously. He reached in his cloak pocket and retrieved two warm crisp bread rolls. "Are you sure about that?"

Pintus, suddenly realizing how unbearably hungry he was, kept one eye on the bread as he replied. "You turned the guards on us! You tried to have Isabella and me killed."

The front guard shook his head vigorously. "I was wrong," he said earnestly. "I wasn't thinking straight. You must believe me, I could never –"

"How did you find us?" interrupted Pintus. He wasn't in the mood to hear the front guard going on and on about how loyal he had really been all along when Pintus had seen for himself what he had done.

"I – I read a fortune cookie," murmured the front guard. He clasped Pintus's hands and looked at him pleadingly. "I feel simply terrible. I could have killed you! Could you ever forgive me?"

"First things first," interrupted Isabella slyly. "The bread?"

The front guard immediately handed them the warm buns. If the light, buttery bread felt warm and comforting in Pintus's hands, it was bliss in his mouth. He stuffed the whole thing into his mouth then let out a grunt of satisfaction as he started swallowing. He ignored the baffled look on the front guard's face, but couldn't help but think of how ridiculous he, the prince, must have looked gobbling down a small roll.

"Water?" asked Isabella with her mouth full.

Looking rattled, the front guard reached into a traveling bag and retrieved a lidded pot of cold water. He handed it to Isabella, who after slurping a good half of it down handed it to Pintus, who drained it in an instant.

Once they had both eaten and drunk their refreshments, Pintus looked at the front guard seriously and untrustingly. "What is the real reason you've come?"

"Well, the fortune cookie also told me –"

"Hang on," said Isabella, "all the stores and shops are closed. The new heir made sure of that. How did you get into the *Enutrof Seikooc*?"

"Oh, it's still open," the front guard assured them. He was still standing before them, but now he crouched down to rest his legs. They didn't have three chairs, and they weren't about to offer theirs for someone who had tried to kill them.

"You see," he continued, "there are many castle workers that oftentimes go to the *Enutrof Seikooc* for guidance, just as I do. The workers would have been infuriated had it been shut down. But back to my story.

"I opened a fortune cookie, and it said: 'A betrayed friend is hiding nearby'. Thinking of you, Pintus, I immediately ordered another cookie, and I read, 'a dangerous noble plan is being plotted'. I wouldn't have thought much of it if it had only said a dangerous plan, but it read a dangerous *noble* plan is being plotted. I knew that somehow the two fortunes related to each other. So I collected some food and water, and went to the building next to the *Enutrof Seikooc*. I felt sure that I could find you. When you weren't behind that building, I went along the backs of all the closed down shops and eventually found you." He leaned forward. "So what's your plan?"

"Are you *mad?* We aren't telling you!" said Isabella indignantly, and Pintus nodded furiously. "You tried to kill us!"

"And I deeply regret it," said the front guard insisted. "Please listen to me. I just want to know when you are going to put it into action!"

"Why on earth would we tell you?" Pintus demanded. "Because you 'deeply regret it'? You would just scurry on back to the castle and tell Queen Lamia. She probably *sent* you here." The very idea terrified Pintus – now Queen Lamia and her cronies would know exactly where the two outcasts were and, if they were to tell him, the castle would know when they planned to break in.

The front guard leaned forward, eyes wide and serious. "I am no longer a part of the castle," he whispered. "Taking an innocent woman like that – and going after children? Absolutely outrageous, and I will never stand for it. I want to help you with the plan." He leaned forward. "You need me. I know the ways of the castle. I know their weaknesses. I could be very useful to you."

Isabella and Pintus looked at each other. "Are you ever going to be returning to the castle?" asked Isabella suspiciously.

"Not unless to go with you to – do whatever it is you are planning to do."

Pintus licked his lips. Isabella looked at him carefully, clearly asking, *should we trust him?* Pintus gave Isabella a significant look, and nodded a tiny fraction of an inch. Isabella returned the gesture.

"All right." said Pintus. "We believe you." Pintus refused to look at him. Isabella glared at the front guard untrustingly.

"So first of all, when are you going to attempt to sneak into the castle?" asked the front guard.

"Early in the morning on the third day," said Isabella.

The front guard looked at them in disbelief. "On the third day? That's madness! The third day is when they are going to burn her!"

"Yes, so we're going to rescue her right before it happens," said Pintus. "We planned it all out perfectly so we have as much time as possible."

"Ridiculous," puffed the front guard. "Look here, we need to do it soon! Not after two days, but immediately!"

"Immediately?" Pintus said in bewilderment. He tried not to glower at him. "But we need time!"

"No, you do not," said the front guard. "Not if planning is unnecessary. You have me now." Pintus could sense the pleasure the front guard took in saying that.

"Unnecessary?" Pintus looked heatedly in Isabella's direction, but she seemed to be thinking along the lines of the front guard.

"I think he's right," she murmured. "Mom needs help now, *before* she's burnt to ashes."

Pintus was now feeling as though no one was listening to him at all.

"I say we do it tomorrow," continued the guard.

Pintus leapt to his feet. "You're *mad!*" he cried out. "You've gone completely mad! Tomorrow? The castle? How can you possibly think that tomorrow is the day we need to –"

"Listen to me," said the front guard.

Isabella reached up and yanked Pintus back into his chair. "He's right," she hissed. "The sooner, the better. . ."

"But what about the mystery? We need time to –"

"We need Mom to figure that out. And think about it – the front guard needs to show us where the dungeon is before we can even find Mom. If we wait for a long time they'll notice that the front guard is missing and be even more cautious and watchful."

Pintus slowly cooled down as the logic took its toll on him. His tense shoulders eased slightly. He knew it made sense, but it still sounded too risky to him. The front guard stood up swiftly from his crouching position. "Excellent," he said. "Tomorrow morning?"

"You're mad," Pintus muttered.

Isabella ignored him. "Not morning," she yawned. "I haven't had a proper night's sleep in days now. How about dusk?"

"I'll be there," promised the front guard. "Where are you two sleeping?"

Isabella and Pintus looked at each other. "You aren't sleeping with us," they said in unison.

The front guard rolled his eyes. "That much I can assume. But I just want to know where to meet you tomorrow morning."

"We'll be right here, at the table." Isabella let out a breath of air, and it visibly rose up into the chilly night air. "For now, though, bedtime."

"Agreed," said Pintus. "Goodbye, front guard."

The front guard hurried off, and Isabella raced, shivering, to open the passageway. Pintus followed, shaking off bits of snow that had fallen on his cloak, doing his best to not think about the approach they were going to take to try to save Mrs. Carole and his kingdom.

Entrance

If just one week ago someone had told Pintus that in less than half a week from that point he would be desperately trying to break into his own castle, he would have told that someone to stop talking nonsense and go find a mental expert in the castle.

Yet there he was, meeting the front guard after a well slept night and taking it gentle until right before evening. The sky was a navy blue color, melting down into different shades of lavender. The cover of the sunset would help them as they attempted to encroach upon the castle. Pintus and Isabella had taken the day easy, not doing much but avoiding the topic of what they were going to do that very evening and trying to make themselves useful in some sort of way. Pintus found that he had made a habit of taking out the locket with the drawing of his father in it, reading the folded up piece of paper containing the poem, and then forcing it all back into the locket before repeating the process once again. He felt restless and nervous, unable to sit down for more than a couple minutes at a time. He couldn't tell if Isabella felt the same way; if she did, she was awfully good at hiding it.

By the time the sun was in the middle of the sky, Pintus felt as if he were about to explode. Hours passed, each seeming to drag along more sluggishly than the last, and then finally the front guard jogged up to the table. Several bricks that they had hastily stuck into the passageway thunked out and fell to the ground. The front guard blinked. Isabella, flushing slightly, hustled to jam a couple of the bricks back into place. The front guard looked at them awkwardly for a moment and then looked quickly away at Pintus. "Good night sleep?" he asked. Pintus nodded. He had to admit, it had been the best night of sleep he had had in some time now.

"Good, because we have an excruciatingly long and challenging evening ahead of us," said the front guard bluntly.

Isabella glowered at the front guard. "Thanks for that comfort," she muttered.

The front guard didn't respond. The sky was clear, and though the air was still chilled, not a cloud could be seen in the sky, and the usual overnight frost seemed to be absent from the scene. Cleven was hopping from one foot to the other in a restless dance. The front guard looked off in the direction of the castle. "We have only a couple hours before the sun will sink. I believe that we need to be in the castle before the sky darkens, because as soon as darkness settles over the land the security tightens an unbelievable amount."

"So where do we enter?" asked Isabella. "Where's their weak spot?"

"By now there should be a different guard in my position," said the front guard, "but there is one place that has been left be." He looked slowly at Pintus. "The Prince's room."

There was silence for a moment. The front guard had sounded quite dramatic but it had basically no meaning to Isabella. "What's the big deal about that?"

"The window," murmured Pintus. "My whole wall . . . it's glass."

"Well, we can't break that glass – it'd make way too loud of a racket," said Isabella.

Pintus nodded in agreement. "Besides, it's tinted. They could see us climbing up to it if a maid went in to clean or something, but we wouldn't see them. That way is far too risky, and this isn't even taking into account the fact that we would have to scale the castle to get up to it."

The front guard licked his lips. "Well, there is one other way."

Pintus and Isabella looked at him eagerly as he began to explain his idea.

"Make sure you put up a big fuss," said the front guard under his breath. He was holding both of them tightly by the wrists, something that made Pintus very nervous. He was dressed, like Isabella, in rags for their entrance. "Are you sure they won't recognize us?" he whispered.

"Trust me, they'll be so focused on the fact that I've caught two criminal children to think about who they look like," the front guard whispered back. They reached the moat, and the front guard waved his arms up and down.

"Bruno!" he called. "Lower the bridge, I've got two thieves here!"

The drawbridge was slowly lowered. The front guard strode across, clenching their elbows. "Shout," he hissed to them. "Put up a fuss!"

Isabella grinned at him. "I'm good at that." She swooned backwards, and started screaming. "Let me *go*, you monster, I'm *innocent*, I'm *innocent!*"

Pintus hastily tried to put up a fuss as well, but he had never needed to throw a tantrum in his life. "Um, we were *framed!* It's all *lies*, we didn't do *anything!*"

The front guard struggled across the bridge with his two squirming allies in hand. "I got two thieves here and I need to bring 'em into the dungeon for questioning," yelled the front guard over the shouts and protests of Isabella and Pintus.

"All right, but hustle up. And be careful," Bruno added in a low voice. "There's a witch down there."

"Of course I'll be careful," said the front guard.

Bruno gave him a sympathetic look as they kept tugging and shrieking that they were innocent. The front guard pulled them into the narrow door leading up the castle. As the door swung shut they all immediately went silent. Pintus's face was now bloodless. They were in the castle.

The only light came from the occasional flickering candle along the stone walls. Wax dribbled down their yellow sides. Pintus had never imagined that his home, a place of comfort and safety, could ever become such a forbidding place. The front guard took a shaky breath. "We're in."

"You were pretty good at screaming your head off, for a prince," snickered Isabella.

Pintus looked around. "So what now?"

"To the dungeon," answered the front guard. "Do you know where that is?" Pintus gazed up at the stairs trailing up the castle. "Below the castle floors. But I don't see any stairs going down . . ." The front guard tapped him on the shoulder and pointed to the left of the stairs. Pintus peered forward. Through the semidarkness he could see a wide wooden board wide enough for two people to stand comfortably on top of. A small black handle curved over it.

"It's a trapdoor!" Pintus exclaimed. He lurched forward and clenched his hand over the handle. Isabella hurried over to help, and together they pulled up the trapdoor and laid it against the wall. Pintus could see now that there was a passageway leading down several curving flights of steps. The stairs were creaky and wooden. A cold, sickening feeling of forbidding seeped inside of Pintus's chest.

"Well, what're you waiting for?" asked the front guard.

Pintus looked at the front guard seriously. "You stay here," he said. "Shout down to us if there's danger. We'll go down, rescue Mrs. Carole, and come back up. Then we'll escape through the castle with her – it'll be easy because we're so close to the entrance."

The front guard nodded swiftly. "Be careful."

"Will there be any guards down there?" asked Isabella.

"Without a doubt," responded the front guard. "The best way to deal with them is to tell them you're a visitor. If they ask for proof, tell them I'm up here waiting. Just . . . just be two little peasant children."

Pintus nodded. He felt that it was desperately risky, considering that he was the prince of the kingdom and had a difficult time imagining that his own guards would not recognize him. But as he looked down at himself he could see that his cloak was so dirty it looked more brown than black, his hands were grimy and cut, and his shoes were worn down and almost unfamiliar to him.

"Good. Thank you, front guard. We'll be on our way." Pintus looked at the front guard meaningfully before turning to the trapdoor. He swallowed, ignoring the throbbing fear that was growing and growing until it became a thumping fear and then a pounding fear and then a thundering fear that grew and grew until –

Isabella gave him a little nudge. "Are you going or not?"

Pintus swallowed again. "I'm going."

He forced one foot forward. Then he slowly rocked his other foot in front of the first. One step after another it became easier and the quicker he walked the more his fear faded. Isabella followed him down, and then the trapdoor clanged shut above them. Pintus felt Isabella duck down.

It was an entirely different world. Everything was damp and dark. The candles were set at closer intervals, but they seemed to be there only to remind them of what a miserable place it was. The stairs wound in wide ovals, and with every downward step the atmosphere became colder and darker. Pintus thought he heard moaning in the distance, and his fingertips tingled with fear.

After what seemed like years, they finally reached the end of the staircase. Isabella's teeth were chattering and Pintus's fingers were quivering from cold. The stairs had come to an end and leveled out to a floor that was nothing more than packed -down dirt. Dirty, caged dungeon cells began to the right of the large, cold room that stretched out before them. Pintus took several tentative steps and peered over into the bars of the first cell. A filthy man was sitting on a bench, glowering menacingly in the twelve-year-olds' direction. Pintus jolted backwards at the look of pure hatred and evil on his face and hurried on to the second cell. But Isabella had beat him to it.

"Nothing there," she whispered. "Just some creeper woman who gave me a look like she wanted to kill me."

Pintus chuckled despite their situation, and shuffled on to the third cell. They looked in, and both immediately leaped backwards. An old, wrinkled, wild-eyed woman was standing inches away from the bars, and she was clutching a long curving knife.

"Ack!" Pintus gasped. "How on earth did she get a hold of *that?*" Though it would have little use inside of the cell, it rather alarmed Pintus to see a dangerous prisoner holding a knife inches away from his face.

Isabella's mouth was wide open, her eyes frozen. "Did I just see a crazy old lady holding a knife in my face?"

Pintus laughed nervously. "Let's go to the next one."

"Hold it right there!" a voice broke through the quiet dungeon. Pintus and Isabella turned around in the direction of the voice. Pintus forced himself to stay calm, mindful that he had to look as though he was supposed to be there, as though there was no reason that he would not be allowed to be there.

From across the dungeon, a fat, grubby man hustled over to them, puffing and huffing. A set of keys jangled at his hip. "What're ye doin' 'ere, eh?!"

Pintus looked at him calmly, and tried to sound like a nervous but innocent peasant boy. "Sorry, sir, but I'm here to visit my – my Aunt."

The man glared at him. "Did anyone give ye permission?"

"Yes, sir. The front guard gave us permission. He's waiting upstairs. You could go up and ask him if you'd like."

The man looked at Pintus as though he was something revolting he had found beneath his shoe. "You two had better not be lyin', or else *you* are gonna be given yesself a cell. Stay *right 'ere.*"

Pintus nodded obediently, and watched with Isabella at his side as the man disappeared up the many steps. As soon as he was out of sight, Pintus hissed, "C'mon, hurry!"

He and Isabella darted to the next cell. They passed several more cells with no familiar faces. Then, finally, at a cell excluded slightly from the others with thicker bars and in an even dirtier state, Isabella let out a cry of joy and rushed to the bars. Pintus, heart wildly banging against his ribs, rushed to her side. Mrs. Carole's face –

dirty, frightened, and bloody, though still familiar – was up against the bars, and tears were running down her face.

"You've come!" she cried. "Oh, you two brave children! *You've come!*"

Truth

Mrs. Carole squeezed her hands between the bars and grasped both Isabella's and Pintus's hands. Isabella had tears of joy in her eyes. They had made it, and now they could rescue Mrs. Carole.

"I . . . I owe you two a large explanation," Mrs. Carole whispered.

"Not now," Pintus said, shaking his head. "We've got to escape first." He looked over at Isabella. "What about the keys?"

"No," insisted Mrs. Carole lurching forward. Her bony body was pressed against the bars as hard as she could possibly do so, straining at them. "No! Please – first let me explain." She seemed as though she was desperate to give them some kind of explanation to justify her actions. Pintus looked at Isabella.

Isabella leaned forward even closer to Mrs. Carole, obviously just as desperate to be near her mother as Mrs. Carole was to be near her. She glanced quickly from her mother to Pintus and back again. "Are . . . are we siblings?"

Mrs. Carole looked from Pintus to Isabella with even more tears sliding down her nose. "Y-Yes. And oh, I never thought I would see you again, Pintus!"

Pintus dug his fingernails into his palm to hold himself together. "But you're dead," he managed. "Father said you were de–"

"Let me start at the beginning. My name is Carole Sanderson. There is no 'Mrs.' about it, though it is a good cover name.

"Your Father was a prince, just around three years older than you are, Pintus. I was a servant girl working in the castle, and I was the one assigned to clean Prince Horace's bedroom – I made his bed every morning, and brought him breakfast. I was never to speak to him unless spoken to. I was never to come within two feet of him *exactly* unless to pick something up or if he gave me permission so I could do some chore."

"You were a servant girl?" said Isabella in amazement.

"Indeed. But let me continue." She took a deep breath. "At the age fourteen, Prince Horace had been assigned a spouse because he had failed to choose one before that age. That spouse was a power-thirsty princess, and though she did not at all love Prince Horace, she was eager to be the queen of the kingdom. This princess was known as Princess Lamia."

"No!" gasped Pintus in amazement. "That's the same name as –"

"I know," said Carole Sanderson, giving him a significant look. "It's the same person too. She was a princess then, and went mad over the thought of the power she could possess. She was absolutely delighted at her opportunity.

"In the meantime, though, Prince Horace had taken to speaking to me. He would tell me of his troubles, realizing that he had found a sympathetic listening ear, and I would relate to them and help him with his difficulties. Before I had realized what had happened, something astounding happened: We fell in love.

"Imagine! A high prince already assigned to marry, in love with a poor servant girl! But though it was a love I had never imagined could exist, it was the best of love there could ever be for both me and Prince Horace.

"After a month, it was time for Prince Horace and Princess Lamia to marry. I was heartbroken. On the day before the wedding, Prince Horace took my hands in his and gently laid a locket with a golden chain into my palm. He told me that no matter what happened that day, he would always love me and he would never go through with the marriage."

Carole Sanderson's eyes were misty. "I waited outside the church door that led to the room where the marriage was taking place, ear pressed up against the door and listening. The priest was droning on, and then after a pause I heard Princess Lamia's sneering voice purr, 'Oh, I do.'

"There was another long buzz of fancy words strung together by the priest, and then there came a shout from inside. It was Prince Horace's voice. 'I do *not!*'

"It sounded like an eruption inside as the crowd around them leapt to their feet. I could hear Princess Lamia's voice shrieking threats and angry words. But Prince Horace's voice rose above all the others. 'I am in love with *Carole Sanderson!* And I will *never* go through with this marriage!'

"I backed away from the door, panicking, just as it was flung open. Prince Horace bolted out. 'Carole!' he cried. 'Run!'"

Isabella's face was white. Pintus's was whiter.

"We ran as fast as we could to the nearest safe place: the woods. We managed to stay in hiding for around a year and a couple weeks, and during that time I had two children, you two. Believe it or not, you were born only hours apart."

Pintus looked in disbelief at Isabella. Her face mirrored his confused and astonished expression.

Looking as though it took all of her strength, Carole Sanderson continued her story, her face pinched with pain. "But then we were discovered by the King, your grandfather. They had been searching for us every minute since we escaped, and at last they had found us. They chose to keep Pintus, because he was a male and therefore the better choice to ascend the throne as king later on, and so they dragged Prince Horace away. They told him that they had killed Isabella and me." Carole Sanderson began to sob. "It – it hurts to think that he believed me to be dead all this time."

"He didn't," said Pintus suddenly.

Carole Sanderson looked at him. Her tears were cutting tracks in the grime on her face. "What d'you mean?"

"He didn't believe you to be dead," said Pintus. "In his will, he left his entire kingdom to you, and put me under your care too. He must have known you were alive."

Carole Sanderson looked at him with a desperate sorrow on her face. "That comforts me more than y-you could ever guess, Pintus," she whispered. "But . . . there's still more to the story.

"Prince Horace refused to marry Princess Lamia even after they had claimed to have killed me. She was furious, and swore to her own grave that she would take revenge on Prince Horace, and that she would make me pay."

Carole's eyes were hard and burning now, blazing with anger. "The castle eventually allowed Prince Horace to become king without a queen, and soon he became one of the best known and fairest king there ever was, despite his haunting past.

"But there was still Princess – now Queen – Lamia. She had sworn to take revenge, and she's living up to her oath as we speak. Now she has killed the king, and plans to burn me. We've got to escape. And we've *got* to save the kingdom."

Pintus was in shock from the story, but it all made sense now. He felt like sobbing, laughing, running, hiding, doing anything to get the wild emotion out. *He had a mother! And. . .* He glanced quickly at Isabella and his heart swelled. *And he had a sister!*

For a moment they all savored their joy and amazement, and then they were snatched rudely back into their situation by a holler down the stairs. "Danger! Daaaaanger!"

The voice bounced down the damp, closed in walls, piercing into Pintus's ears. His heart jumped to his throat in terror. It was the front guard's voice, and Pintus remembered immediately that he had told him to call down to them if something went wrong. Panic rose in his stomach. Isabella whirled around to stare in horror at Pintus.

Carole Sanderson yelped, "The keys! They're over there, right across from this cell, hanging on the wall! They put them there to taunt me, I remember Queen Lamia insisting on them being right there in my sight."

Pintus darted across the room, and grabbed the ring of large, rusty keys. He ran back, the front guard's voice still echoing down the many stairs, and gasped, "Do you remember which key they locked you with?"

"No, I fell unconscious!"

Pintus, heart banging so hard in his chest that it was painful, jammed a random key into the slot and turned it. There was no result. He shoved another one in, and another. He could hear the front guard's voice, still screaming from the top that danger was coming, and then a loud banging noise and silence. Pintus's fingers froze on the lock.

Isabella leapt into his place and kept pushing in keys. Her fingers were shaking so badly it was making the lock rattle. She pressed in another key, and at long last the lock broke open in her hands. It clattered to the floor and Pintus scrambled to swing the door wide.

"Oh, my babes!" cried out Carole Sanderson, and she burst out and wrapped her arms around them. Pintus felt hot tears building up behind his eyes. He immediately blinked hard and swallowed rapidly.

"Come on, we've gotta go!" she said.

They ran for the steps. It was a much more exhausting trek, running up the stairs. Pintus could hear muffled voices and clanging noise that sounded like metal against metal. They kept running, Carole Sanderson keeping up the rear, and finally they reached the last flight of steps. Pintus could see from the flickering orange light of the candles that they were only feet away from the trapdoor . . . but the trapdoor was shut.

"That was what the banging noise was," he groaned. "Whatever the danger was, it locked us down here!"

"Not necessarily locked," said Carole Sanderson, and she lurched forward, arms outstretched. Isabella hurried to help her, and together the small broken family rammed up against the trapdoor. It vibrated and dented upwards, but the sides held fast. "Again!" Isabella shouted. They all took a step back and once more charged at the trapdoor above them. It was weakening – Pintus could see the hinges beginning to bust apart.

"One more time!" Pintus yelled, and this time the trapdoor was sent flying backwards. "C'mon!"

They struggled out of the hole where the trapdoor was, and looked around the small space. It was completely trashed. The crank for the drawbridge was dented and broken. The trapdoor they had just defeated was flung backwards and was smashed against the wall. The door leading outside to the moat was hanging by one hinge. The candles were deformed, sliced in places, as though swords had missed their targets and skimmed over the surface of the wax.

"No one's here!" Isabella cried. "I think we can make it! C'mon, let's go, quick!"

"I wouldn't suggest that," came a dark venomous voice from the stairs above them.

Pintus turned around.

Darold

Pintus could tell immediately, with a heart-stopping jolt, that there were at least twelve guards all heavily armored and all holding spears or swords, gathered at the foot of the many steps leading upwards. Isabella let out a groan of frustration. Pintus was too shocked to speak. A bead of sweat gathered at the top of his forehead, and he swiped it away with one hand. Carole Sanderson was the only one able to keep her composure – or seemed to keep her composure.

At the front of the group a single man, probably the leader, stood, and Pintus could tell that he had been the one speaking. His eyes gleamed evilly above his black drooping mustache. Pintus's eyes scanned over the group, searching for the front guard and found him blended into the group. At first Pintus felt a rush of anger and betrayal, but then the front guard gave him a small nondescript nod, and Pintus's anger eased slightly.

"Oh, such a *sad* story," drawled the leader in a nasty voice dripping in sarcasm. "Almost freed – almost able to escape, and caught just on the homestretch. Well,

Sanderson, *you* at least should know that Queen Lamia never fails."

He looked mockingly at Carole Sanderson, who kept her dignity and stared shamelessly straight back into his cold eyes. Not one word was necessary. There was a moment of loathing silence and then the leader's eyes darted away from hers.

"On the subject of failing, I'm afraid you few have reached the end of the line." A crooked smile was on his face now, such a smile that Pintus wanted to give that leader a good slug in the face, an emotion that would have been despicable to him just days ago.

"This witch will be taken back," he snarled triumphantly, eyes flickering briefly in Carole Sanderson's direction and then coming back to rest again on Pintus, "and not only that, but with two other criminals!" He paused. "But I doubt you'll go down without a fight."

"*Never!*" Pintus and Isabella shouted together.

"Excellent," sneered the leader, and then opened his mouth to bellow the signal when suddenly there came a yell from inside the small crowd of guards. *"Prince Pintus shall prevail!"*

A sword came slashing down through the air, missing the leader by inches. The leader let out a roar of fury, and immediately lunged at the front guard, who suddenly reached into his belt and flipped two shiny daggers out into the fingers of his left hand. "Pintus! Isabella!"

"What're you waiting for, you fools?!" screamed the leader. The group of guards was still on the staircase, waiting for the signal. *"Get them!"*

The front guard, still holding the long silver sword, let out a yell as the armed guards swarmed to him, waving their weapons. The small space was ridiculously crowded now with raving soldiers.

Pintus whirled and looked around with crazed eyes for some kind of escape, but there was only one way out – up.

"C'mon!" He grabbed Isabella's hand, and fought his way through the crowd, defending himself the best he could as guards sliced their swords at him. Some seemed slightly hesitant to hit a woman and two children, but they were not about to disobey orders, and soon Pintus was smeared with blood and barely able to hold onto Isabella's slipping fingers. He was only feet away from the stairs, pushing his way through the many bodies when suddenly a rough hand dug into his arm.

"Don't try to escape," growled a low, snarling voice, and a sword blade was laid delicately against Pintus's arm, "or I press."

"*Isabella, run!*"

"Pintus!" The front guard, somehow seeming to have escaped, exploded out of nowhere and crashed into the guard who had the sword against Pintus's arm. The guard was flung in the opposite direction.

Carole Sanderson screamed, "The stairs!"

They bolted for the stairs, Carole Sanderson in front, then Isabella and Pintus, with the front guard keeping up the rear. The battling guards seemed to take a second to realize that their victims were running up and away, they were so involved in fighting through each other and arguing in rowdy voices.

Carole, Pintus, and Isabella had almost reached the first upward curve of the stairs and escaped from the soldiers' sight when suddenly the guard that the front guard had shoved away from Pintus looked up from the ground where he had landed. Pintus twisted around in mid-run. The sword that the grounded guard had thrown seemed to fly in slow motion as it sped in perfect aim for its target. Pintus strained to scream a desperate warning to the victim, but horror choked off the sound as the spinning sword hit the target squarely in the back.

The front guard soared forward, mouth jutted open in shock, eyes wide and disbelieving, and sailed to the ground at the foot of the stairs. His chin hit the stone steps solidly as he crumpled. Pintus opened his mouth to scream out, but no sound could escape.

"Isabella!" he finally managed to rasp.

She turned around and froze, shock and terror in her eyes.

Beyond the front guard's body the chasing guards had begun to notice their absence, and seeing them at the stairs, began shouting and swarming up at the bottom.

"Isabella, help me pick him up!" Pintus gasped. "We can carry him to safety!"

"Pintus – Pintus we can't, they're coming, he's too far gone – we could never save him!"

"No! We can carry him, help me, take his feet, he'll survive if we just –" But he knew there was no point. Isabella would not have tears whelming up in her eyes if it wasn't true, if the front guard really could survive. The guards were starting up the stairs now, their armor clanging.

But Pintus couldn't bring himself to run from them. He had realized, with a sharp pain in his chest and a building hotness in his eyes, that this may be the last time he would ever see life in the front guard's eyes. Pain swelled inside of him. He forced himself to take one wobbly step down the stairs. Then another. A couple more and he was at the front guard's side.

"Pintus –" warned Isabella. Her voice was strangled by sorrow.

But Pintus couldn't stop now. They were losing their headstart on the guards, but he didn't care now. He bent down next to the front guard, took a deep shaky breath, and looked deep into the front guard's fading eyes. A lump throbbed in his throat.

"Front guard," he whispered in a choked voice he was hardly able to control, "what's your name?"

The front guard gave a distant smile. "Darold," he told him. It was the last word Pintus heard him speak. A single tear collected in the corner of Pintus's eye and slowly rolled down his cheek before landing on the front guard's colorless face.

Isabella snatched Pintus's hand and dragged him to his feet. "C'mon, Pintus," she gasped. " We've – we've got to keep running!"

Pintus could feel the bellows and threats of the guards, the sound of the many feet pounding against the cold stone, and his own blind sobs racking over his body, but all he could hear over and over again was *Darold, Darold, Darold*.

Outrunning

The guards thundered up the stairs. Carole Sanderson, Isabella, and Pintus could barely stay out of their reach. Isabella was still pulling Pintus along, who was hunched over, breathing hard and fast, trying to shake off the image of Darold's blank eyes.

Cold.

Dark.

Darold.

Crashing metal. Screaming threats.

Darold.

"Pintus! *Pintus!*" Isabella yanked him foreword. "I can't keep pulling you, it takes too much time! Pintus!" Losing her patience, Isabella slapped him clear across the face and yelled, "PINTUS!"

Pintus's head snapped up. Reality came into a sharp focus. It took a lot of effort not to sink back into his suffocating despair.

"What?"

"What d'you think?" Isabella screamed at him. *"They're trying to kill us!* I can't keep pulling you!"

A spear whizzed by Isabella, missing her head by inches. Pintus could feel the rush of air as it passed. He ripped his hand out of Isabella's, anger surging through him. They had killed his father, captured his mother, and killed his friend, but he would never, *never* let them have his sister!

"You always feel the most alive when you're closest to death," King Horace had once told Pintus, and at this point he couldn't agree more. Pintus wheeled around and sprinted up the stairs with a new energy, calling for Isabella to come too. He wasn't going to be the one who held them back, he would make sure of that.

"Yes!" Isabella shouted triumphantly, running after him. She passed him almost immediately, the muscles in her thin legs rippling, but Pintus could easily keep up.

They immediately started putting some distance between the yelling guards and themselves, Carole Sanderson at the front and Pintus in the back. They whirled around the next curve, slowly but surely making the small space between them and the wrath of the guards widen. Pintus felt unbearably trapped – what other way out of the castle was there?

His legs felt heavier with every pace, but he ignored the pain easily so that he hardly felt it as his newly strengthened legs flashed back and forth, climbing up to safety. The horror, despair, fright, exhilaration, hope, and a thousand other confusing painful emotions all mixed together into one giant energy flowed through him at such a rate that he couldn't stop running. He had to get it out, he had to free himself.

They rounded the next curve and for a split second they couldn't see the guards. It was their chance.

"Here!" Carole Sanderson dove for the closest door.

Pintus and Isabella threw themselves in after her and found themselves in the middle of a long hallway branching off on both sides of them. A large, wide room was in front of them, with a glass door leading to another room. Pintus leapt to his feet and kicked the door shut. Isabella climbed to her feet. Pintus slowly slid to the ground, trembling. Isabella sat down next to him. Blood trickled down her cheek and she clutched the dagger the front guard had thrown to her as though her life depended on it – which very well could have been true.

"Where are we?" whispered Carole Sanderson.

Pintus looked around. "Well, I know that the door over there" He pointed to the door at the end of the room in front of him. "leads to the balcony that overlooks the kingdom. My father used to go there for his speeches. It's actually a good amount of space – one time we had some dancers perform for the citizens out there."

"Is it a safe place?" asked Isabella tensely.

"Not now," answered Pintus grimly. "Everyone's against us."

They didn't speak for a moment. They could hear the guards thundering up to the floor they were on. They waited silently, the suspense so thick in the air that they could almost see it.

"Keep running, you lazy fools! Catch them! *Catch them!*" the leader's voice barked at the guards.

Despite their desperate situation, Pintus couldn't help but wonder how Cleven was doing. It felt strange not to have him swaying on his shoulder, giving him unwavering comfort in times of fear like these. But he knew it was safest that they had left him in the hideout.

After several minutes the shouting subsided. But even when the sound faded, they still waited tensely, barely daring to breathe.

Finally Isabella whispered, "I think they went to the next floor."

Pintus stood. "We can go back down and escape over the moat!" he said excitedly. His heart was already lightening. If they could escape, if they could make it out and save Carole Sanderson, it would be all worth it, none of the rest would matter –

Carole Sanderson and Isabella were at Pintus's side at once. Pintus grabbed the door handle leading back to the stairs and pulled.

Clink.

The door opened a crack, and Pintus could see with a sudden wave of dread that the door was bolted. *Bolted!* A small strong chain threaded the door and the wall next to it together. Pintus felt his entire body go cold. They were trapped.

"Who bolted it?" Isabella's voice was a whisper of shock.

Carole Sanderson licked her lips. "One of the guards must've," she said.

Pintus tried to hold himself together. "Okay. Let's go down the hallway." He nodded briefly towards the right of the hallway they were standing in. "C'mon. To the right."

Isabella shook her head. "No, I don't think that's going to help us. We'll just get lost in the castle."

Pintus threw his dagger onto the floor with such force that it bounced and reflected the candlelight for a glimmer of a second before it landed still. "Then what're we going to do? We were *this* close to escaping, and now we're trapped!" He held his pointer finger and his thumb a centimeter apart to emphasize how close they were.

He ran his fingers through his hair, unable to grasp how they could be locked in at the very time they so desperately needed to get out.

"P-Prince Pintus?"

Pintus froze.

"P-Prince Pintus, is that y-you?"

The faint trembling voice had come from the left of Pintus. He slowly turned, his thumbnail digging into his palm. The voice sounded vaguely familiar. He bent down to pick up the dagger he had thrown down in frustration, and slowly made his way to the direction of the voice.

"P-Prince?"

Pintus paused. The voice had come from behind the door to a large luxurious bathroom. Pintus's hand reached out and closed over the golden doorknob. Isabella touched his shoulder in warning. Pintus nodded to acknowledge her, but did not release the doorknob. He felt there was something important beyond it, and he couldn't go on without knowing whose voice was calling him.

Pintus twisted the knob and flung the door open.

"P-Prince Pintus, it *is* you!"

"Mr. Cane!" yelped Pintus.

And indeed, chained to the floor between two parallel mirrors so his reflection bounced off the walls over and over again, was a bloody, disheveled man with glasses that perched on the edge of his nose and gray hair that grew only on the sides of his head, leaving the middle bald, a man that Pintus knew to be Mr. Cane. Pintus rushed to his side, hastily tucking the dagger back into his pocket.

"Mr. Cane, are you all right?" Pintus asked, fingers fumbling over the metal chains locking him to the ground. "How'd you get here?"

"P-Prince Pintus. . ." Mr. Cane reached out a weak, wrinkled arm towards Pintus as far as the chain would allow him. His fingers closed over Pintus's wrist. His eyes were wild, and Pintus couldn't help but notice the stammer he had developed. "P-Prince Pintus – you need to – you need –"

"Mr. Cane, don't worry. You're fine, you'll be okay, you can come with us now," Pintus said soothingly. "Now, where are the keys for those chains?"

Isabella jingled the ring of dungeon keys still encircling her wrist and stepped forward to Mr. Cane.

The grip Mr. Cane had on Pintus's wrist tightened. "P-Prince, you n-need to g-g-go! N-Now! G-Go, P-Prince, p-please!"

Pintus patted his back gently. His heart jolted as he felt the rips in Mr. Cane's shirt and the dried blood that coated them. "Mr. Cane, your back. . ."

Mr. Cane gasped in pain at Pintus's touch. Then, with eyes full of pain and terror, he jerked Pintus's hand off his shoulder and shouted, *"G-Go! P-Pintus, go! G-Go now,* th-they're coming, th-they've always b-been coming _"

"Who's coming?" Pintus said desperately. "What're you talking about?"

Isabella shoved a key into the lock. It snapped open and she dove to unlock Mr. Cane. Pintus hurried to help her detangle him from the sharp chains. The whole time Mr. Cane gasped desperate warnings to them.

Mr. Cane's knotty fingers curled over Pintus's hand like a claw. Pintus forced himself to turn and look at him. The look in his eyes was something Pintus would never forget. Beads of sweat glistened on Mr. Cane's colorless lips. As though it took all the energy in the world, they slowly opened to form one word.

Run.

Death Threat

"Pintus!" Isabella's sharp cry of warning cut through the empty air.

Pintus jumped to his feet and whirled around. The sharp clanking noises and rowdy shouting voices coming from behind the bathroom door were unmistakable. Mr. Cane had been warning him. The guards were coming, and they were coming fast.

"C'mon!" Pintus dove for the freed Mr. Cane and swung his frail arm over his shoulder. He looked quickly over at Isabella and Carole Sanderson. "We're taking him with us!"

Mr. Cane struggled as ferociously as an old beaten man could. "N-No! No!"

Isabella ran to Pintus's side and grabbed Mr. Cane's other arm. He pulled back and gasped, "N-No! Y-You'll be h-held back, n-no! L-Leave –"

"We are *not* leaving you behind," Pintus said angrily. "Now come *on*, we're wasting time, we've got to escape!"

"I believe it's a little late for that," came an icy voice from the bathroom door.

Pintus looked up from Mr. Cane's pale face. Queen Lamia was standing in the doorframe, a sharp silver knife in her hand and with her entire group of bloodthirsty knights arranged behind her.

"You!" spat Carole Sanderson, face rigid with hatred.

"Me," said Queen Lamia calmly, her cold eyes now focused on her enemy's face. There was a pause during which both of them glowered venomously at one another, Carole Sanderson's eyes fiery and Queen Lamia's cold. Then Queen Lamia's eyes darted to Pintus, Mr. Cane, and Isabella.

"Don't waste your time, Prince," Queen Lamia snarled to Pintus. "Don't soil your cloak." She took a smart step directly towards him. "You don't need these commoners."

What was she talking about?

"Besides, who are you to think you can possibly win a battle against me and my entire staff of knights –" With a flourish she waved towards the guards behind her, and they all banged their swords and spears to the ground in unison. "– with a little old lady, a child, and a weak old man?"

Pintus felt Mr. Cane's arm stiffen around his shoulder.

Queen Lamia took another step closer to him. "I know about your past," she said in a soft deadly whisper. "I know your family's darkest secrets. I know things that, if you continue on your current path, you will never know about your mother, your father, and you." Her words hung in the air.

"Don't listen to her, Pintus!" screamed Isabella.

"Come," said Queen Lamia in that same soft, evil voice. "Join us."

Pintus's body seemed to have frozen. He could hear his pulse in his ears. The world was silent around him.

"Why do you want me?" He felt his lips moving to form the words, could hear his own voice speaking it, but was unaware of his thought process. As he stared into Queen Lamia's heartless eyes, though, he felt a surge of fury that snapped him back to reality. He took a huge step forward, straight at Queen Lamia. His mind was coming back into focus, and his voice was angry now. "To manipulate me? To kill me while I'm turned the other way?"

He closed the space between them so her livid face was a mere inch from his. "I'd rather die now."

"Perfect," Queen Lamia said, and with a slashing lunge, ripped the shining knife above her head. It paused there, as though she was waiting for him to cry out for her forgiveness. Her eyes focused on Pintus's face. Pintus refused to flinch.

Then, just as Queen Lamia was about to bring the knife down upon Pintus's head, Mr. Cane slumped against Pintus. Pintus whirled to see why – and realized Isabella had let go of his left arm and was lunging for Queen Lamia.

"Isabella, *no!*"

But it was too late. Isabella dove for Queen Lamia's knees and hit them hard. Queen Lamia buckled on top of her, arms flailing, the knife flying out of her hands to send a crack erupting through the mirror.

Isabella shoved the woman off her and bolted for the bathroom door. Carole Sanderson and Pintus ran after her, Pintus leaving Mr. Cane behind with the logic that to bring him would be to drag him into even more danger.

Isabella wrestled her way through the crowd of confused and angry knights. Just as Pintus broke through the group, a shout arose.

"THEY DARE ASSAULT HER HIGHNESS! GET THEM! *GET THEM!*"

It was the leader.

A guard's arm swooped out and seized Pintus by the cloak. Pintus, fear jumping in his chest, wrenched it free, and like a cat dodging an angry dog's jaws, sprinted after Isabella and Carole Sanderson. Isabella was running for the balcony door. Carole Sanderson got there first and flung the door open. The frigid air gusted in Pintus's overheated face as he skidded out onto the balcony.

Gray storm clouds rolled above them, dark and forbidding. Frozen chunks of snow and ice fell upon the balcony. Pintus could see his breath as he whirled around to kick the door shut as hard as he could.

"How much time did that buy us?" he shouted.

"Not much," Carole Sanderson shouted back over the roar of the wind.

"What're we going to do now? We're cornered – trapped!" Pintus moaned.

"Not necessarily," said Isabella, and Pintus saw her eyes stray down to the ground beneath them.

"Absolutely not," said Carole Sanderson immediately. The door was giving way. Pintus's heart rate accelerated. "There's nothing to break our fall down there."

Pintus let out a shaky breath of air. "Then we'll fight and defend ourselves to get out of this, or we'll die trying."

Isabella's lip quivered. Pintus reached out and gave her hand a gentle squeeze. "We'll never stop fighting."

Carole Sanderson laid her arms over both of her children. "Never," she agreed.

Balcony

There was one last pound against the door, and then the whole thing came smashing down at Pintus, Isabella, and Carole Sanderson's feet, swords and spears stuck into the wood. Isabella screamed. Pintus held his breath, forcing to silence the scream that rose in his throat. The guards were so close – too close – they could be thrown off the balcony any second.

Queen Lamia's mouth curved up in a triumphant smile, and the group exploded at them. Pintus dove forward and down onto the broken door, suffering the stampeding feet of his heavy enemies. He scrabbled with his hands to grasp one of the spears stuck in the door. He could hear Isabella shouting and Carole Sanderson fighting, but all that mattered was that he could separate that spear from the tough wood.

"Oh, no ye don't!" A guard's smelly breath clouded into Pintus's nose, and a particularly nasty man boldly swung his arms around Pintus's torso and yanked him upwards.

Rage suddenly took control of Pintus – rage such as he had never before felt in his life, spitting and boiling inside of him, coloring his face and making his heart pound wildly for a different cause. *His own guard* was crudely lifting him up by his stomach! The disrespect was enough to make Pintus want to explode in anger. He lunged his arms out, and his fingertips barely closed over the top of a spear sticking out of the door. He gave it an almighty wrench, the fury strengthening him, and kicked out with his legs, managing to hit the guard in the stomach.

The clanging of armor told Pintus that he had not dealt the fatal blow as he wished, but the guard was so infuriated by his intention that he rose up and flung Pintus to the ground.

The breath knocked out of him, flat on his back and with a sword to his chest, Pintus prepared to say his goodbyes to the world. Then, at that very moment, he recognized the guard who was about to kill him.

And as he realized it, he saw Darold's empty eyes and the round tears rolling down Isabella's cheek and Pintus forcing himself to run. . .

"*You!*" His voice came out as a scream. A hoarse, exploding scream full of anger and grief and hatred.

Pintus yanked the spear out from under his arm and sent it flailing at the guard. It sliced through the armor into the guard's arm, leaving a scarlet line on his skin and a red splotch on Pintus's spear. The guard was so shocked that Pintus was able to struggle out of his grasp and leap to his feet.

Pintus grasped the spear tight in his hands, ready to hurt the evil guard as badly as he possibly could, ready to *kill* him, ready to – to –

"Pintus!" Isabella's voice was full of terror.

Pintus whirled. "Isabella?"

Isabella was held down by three guards at once, and one was raising a sword. Pintus ran. Instantly he forgot about the guard, forgot about Darold, forgot about everything but closing the space between him and his sister who needed him. He tackled the guard raising the sword, his slight body managing to knock him over by the anger that drove him so strongly. He shoved him aside and ran for Isabella.

"You monsters!" he yelled at the guards. "How dare you? How can you *live* with yourselves, loyally serving me for so long and now seeking to destroy my family!"

For a moment they stared at him, obviously shocked by his outburst. Then, suddenly, one of them shouted out in pain and snapped his hand up. Stuck into the metal armor and obviously into the flesh beneath, was Isabella's dagger.

"Yah!" Isabella ripped up her other hand from the two remaining guards, swung around backwards in an impressive flip, and knocked them both senseless with a wild, flailing kick to their heads.

Pintus blinked. He suddenly felt very glad he had never gotten into a fight with Isabella.

Queen Lamia wasn't even fighting. She was simply standing in the doorway, watching with a smug sneer on her face. Every time they sent a guard to the ground, disbelief would flash briefly in her eyes, but it was gone almost as soon as it appeared. Finally, as an eighth guard slumped to the ground at the hands of Carole Sanderson, she screamed, "Enough socializing! Half of you go for Sanderson, everyone else nail the children!"

Carole Sanderson was fighting terrifically. Pintus had to wonder where on earth she learned to handle a sword, because she was whipping it back and forth at the guards so fast it was only a blur, and even the best of the guards was no match for her. But she still wasn't good enough to take on the pack of eight top-trained guards running at her, brandishing swords and screeching threats.

"C'mon!" Pintus said to Isabella. "We've got to help her!"

"Business before pleasure, my *dear* brother, business before pleasure!" Isabella shouted back sarcastically, pointing towards the guards thundering towards them.

"Right," said Pintus, shifting from foot to foot as the guards running towards them neared closer and closer. He tightened his grip on his spear. "What do we. . .?"

"Pintus," Isabella murmured out of the corner of her mouth, "When I say *now*, jump as far as you can to the left and get low." She was backing slowly away from the guards, towards the balcony's railing.

"What –?" Pintus began.

"Just. Trust. Me," hissed Isabella, hands curling over the top of the railing and facing the oncoming guards with a look of pure determination upon her face.

Pintus had a hundred questions and a hundred fears, but he just nodded tightly as the guards thundered loudly and dangerously towards them, dirty greedy faces alight in evil eagerness.

Pintus looked at Isabella. He could hardly breathe for fear. But Isabella looked cool and calm as the guards drew their swords and waved them inches from her face. They were so close Pintus could smell the iron of their armor when Isabella yelled, "Now!"

Pintus threw himself as far to the left as he could, landing hard on his stomach and clamping his hands over his neck to protect himself from the guards. He could hear them shouting and banging when Pintus suddenly realized Isabella's intention.

"Stop! Stop!" yelped one of the guards.

But it was too late. One – two – three – *four* guards had been coming too fast at Pintus and Isabella and were now buckling over the railing and flying off the balcony to their doom.

"Stop, you fools!" hollered a guard.

"Who's the fool?" Isabella's voice said, and then the guard's scream of fear and shock echoed in Pintus's ear as Isabella nudged the faltering guard off the balcony.

Pintus looked up.

Now Isabella was skillfully sword fighting with another guard. She glanced at Pintus. "Go help Mom!"

Pintus didn't hesitate. Carole Sanderson was fighting hard, clothes ripped, face smeared with blood, and her sword slashing. But there were just too many guards. The sheer number of them all was overcoming her. He ran to help her.

When he reached the group of guards surrounding his mother, he gripped his spear hard and yelled, "Hey! Hey, over here!"

Eight heads turned to look at him. Carole Sanderson, taking advantage of their distraction, sent a guard to the ground with a sword stuck through the armor. Another came at her, but Carole simply wrenched the helmet off the dead guard and thrust it hard against the attacker's head. He crumpled.

Pintus, trying to shake that nauseating image, fought to his mother's side.

"I'm here," he said, clinking his spear against a guard's sword.

"So I noticed. Thanks for distracting 'em," Carole Sanderson said, ducking. A sword sliced through the air exactly where her neck had been a second ago.

"You're welcome. Where's Lamia?"

"You dare speak her name with such disrespect?" howled a guard in disgust.

Pintus fought off the guard while Carole Sanderson replied, "Still in the doorframe, I think. She's furious! She's not even trying to hide it anymore."

Pintus glanced over at her and shuddered. Queen Lamia was standing there, a rigid column, eyes burning in anger.

"Wait a minute – she's coming out of the doorframe!" Pintus exclaimed.

Carole Sanderson froze. A guard, taking advantage of that, lunged forward, but Pintus sent him reeling to the ground before the blade touched her. The guard clutched the gap in his armor and fell to the ground.

"I think. . ." Carole Sanderson whispered, "I think she's coming out to fight!"

Pintus looked away from the guard on the ground and over towards the now-empty doorframe. Queen Lamia was striding confidently forward amongst her fighting guards. She seemed to be taking in everything – Pintus and Carole Sanderson fighting her many guards, and Isabella one-handedly outsmarting the remaining guards. She made a beeline for Isabella.

Isabella was clashing with the guard that Pintus recognized immediately as Darold's killer. Pintus's hands tightened over his spear.

"Pintus, look out –" Carole Sanderson yelped, quickly fending off a guard.

"Sorry. . ." Pintus couldn't stop watching now.

Queen Lamia was approaching Isabella's opponent. Snowflakes landed to rest on her eyelashes. She paused behind the guard, almost as though she were simply stopping to listen to the sharp *clank, clank, clank* of the two fighters' swords. Then she slowly and delicately reached into her cloak pocket to pull out a small, sharp dagger. In one fluid movement she stabbed the guard fighting Isabella smoothly in the back.

Edge

Pintus caught a glimpse of the evil man's shocked eyes before he fell face-first onto the ice-glazed wood of the balcony. He whirled to block one of the fighting guards, but his mind was still on Queen Lamia's brutal act.

Queen Lamia yanked the dead guard's sword from his stiff fingers. For a moment she examined it almost lazily in her hands. Then she roughly kicked the guard's body aside and moved in on Isabella. Pintus's face whitened.

"Can you handle it over here?" he asked Carole Sanderson.

"Yes – go, go!" Carole cried back.

Pintus broke away from the guards and ran for Isabella. Isabella was faring well so far – ducking skillfully and jabbing out at Queen Lamia with her sword. Pintus could see the anger building up behind his sister's brown-black eyes as her opponent took another slash through the air with the sword she had so heartlessly stolen from her own guard.

Pintus had to admit, though, the Queen was a skilled fighter. She was fast to block a blow and just as fast to deliver – her sword sliced through the air with terrifying accuracy. Her face had a sort of messy, reckless fury, as though she was willing to do anything to get that sword into Isabella's chest.

Pintus stopped and watched for a moment, trying to figure out how to predict Queen Lamia's strategies.

Isabella was doing a lot of wild rolls, ducking, and vain swiping with her sword. Her knuckles were bleeding and her dirty hair was even grimier and tangled than usual as she darted back and forth, sword in hand, trying to evade and attack over and over again, evade and attack, evade and attack. Her strategy seemed to be making Queen Lamia even more frustrated and angry with every move.

Queen Lamia was harder to figure out. She was constantly and unpredictably lunging out with her sword, making long, dangerous swooping motions with it that Isabella could barely avoid. But Pintus could never guess when she would leap into an attack – she would be fighting defensively one minute, and then viciously attacking the next.

"Isabella!" Pintus couldn't stand waiting a second longer. He wasn't about to let Carole Sanderson and Isabella do all of the fighting – they needed him. "I'm coming!"

"Glad you finally came to help!" Isabella shouted over the clang of metal as her sword made contact with Queen Lamia's sword. "I thought you'd never –" Her voice cut off sharply. Queen Lamia had taken a wild jab with her sword at Isabella while it was still vibrating, catching Isabella off guard.

Pintus rushed to cover her. "Well, I'm here now," he said.

"What does it matter anyway?" screamed Queen Lamia. "You'll both be dead when I'm finished with you!"

Isabella swiped her sword furiously at Queen Lamia. She didn't need to say a word. The intensity with which she fought and the hatred within her eyes said it all.

"I'm sick of this!" the evil woman screamed. "I'm ending it *now!*"

Her sword whipped high into the air and with crushing speed, slammed down at them.

To Pintus, the sword seemed to streak through the air in slow motion. The metal gleamed in the crisp, weak sunshine. His entire world revolved around that moment. And in that moment he made a decision.

"Isabella, duck!"

Pintus threw himself to the ground and dove straight between Queen Lamia's legs. The ice on the balcony cut into his fingers as he slid beneath her in a straight line. Just before he came back out from under her he banged his legs as hard as he could into hers and gave her backside a push so strong that she completely lost her balance. All of his rage and strength exploded out of him as he shoved her.

Pintus had really just been hoping for her to get off balance, but she had somehow slammed straight against the edge of the balcony. She had barely managed not to soar over it, and was now clinging to the railing, the upper part of her body suspended in the blustery wind, her face white from cold and – could it be? – fear. Her sword went over the edge, shimmering off the reflection from the sun as it fell. She was shrieking in rage, halfway keeled over the railing, but Pintus and Isabella could only hear streams of fractured words and parts of sentences as the wind whirled away the sound of her spitting fury.

Pintus and Isabella looked at each other and silently nodded. Pintus turned to where Pintus's mother, Carole Sanderson, was fighting, and whistled sharply so she looked up. Isabella vigorously motioned her over. The guards looked frozen as they stared at their leader's figure on the railing.

Carole Sanderson slowly walked towards them, her feet making loud crunching noises on the balcony's snow. Not one guard moved.

Isabella and Pintus had Queen Lamia cornered on the edge. She was leaning so far over that her legs weren't touching the balcony. She was struggling viciously to regain her footing, but Pintus and Isabella weren't about to allow that.

Carole Sanderson approached them. "Yes?"

"Would you like to do the honors?" he asked. He felt jittery and slightly nauseous.

Carole Sanderson gave him a modest smile. "I would love that," she said. She strode slowly between Pintus and Isabella, toward Queen Lamia. She leaned down close to her enemy's face.

"There is still a chance," she whispered. "You could start anew in the castle. You could change. It doesn't have to end this way."

"Mom –" Isabella began.

Carole Sanderson repeated, "It doesn't have to end this way."

Queen Lamia's face contorted and flushed bright red. "I'd rather die!" she snarled. "You just wait, Sanderson! It may not be this time, but I will have my revenge!"

Carole Sanderson spoke slowly and deliberately, each word angry and serious. "Very well." She paused. "But you will *never* hurt another innocent soul again."

And with that, Carole Sanderson stepped away from Queen Lamia. She took three large, measured steps back from her, and then gave a curt nod to Pintus and Isabella. They stepped away.

Carole Sanderson sprinted forward and thrust her arms out. They smacked against Queen Lamia, who let out a scream of fury as she toppled off the side of the railing and plunged into the vast space below.

Pintus leaned over, his heart pounding in his mouth, and watched Queen Lamia shrink smaller and smaller until she was nothing but a speck and then nothingness as she neared the ground. For a long moment he just stood there, Isabella's shoulder against his own, hardly daring to believe that it was finally, finally over.

Then the tears came, hot and uncontrollable, welling up his eyes and then squeezing out in bursts of pain and sorrow. They ran down Pintus's face and froze as they hit the balcony ground. Isabella was crying too – Pintus felt her shoulders shaking. He grabbed her hand and squeezed it tight, gasping for his own breath, eyes closed tight. Then Carole Sanderson's arms closed over both of them, warm and protecting.

Her voice whispered through the tears, "I love you . . . I love you both . . . so. . . so much . . ."

Pintus buried his face in her warmth. When he looked up again, he realized that all of the remaining guards were sinking to their knees. Removing their helmets. Bowing their heads.

"Prince Pintus," the one closest to him murmured, "Welcome back."

Pintus's Kingdom

"Good to *see* you, Pintus!"

"I *did* miss you, how *marvelous* it is for you to be back!"

"I must say, I was *quite* worried. . ."

It was the strangest thing for Pintus to re-enter the castle and have everyone happily welcoming him and opening doors for him. Cleven flew through the door and nestled onto Pintus's shoulder. Pintus reached up and gave his owl a gentle stroke on his back. Then he made his way to the bathroom where Mr. Cane was still lying.

Isabella was looking at every guard with suspicion, distrust. Her face was filthy with dirt and blood, her hair tangled beyond repair. Carole Sanderson looked pretty rough, too, bloody and dirty, but her eyes were dancing with joy.

"Wait here," said Pintus to the guards as they neared the bathroom door. With his family at his side, he slipped into the bathroom.

"Oh, P-Prince Pintus, you're all r-right!" Mr. Cane cried.

"Mr. Cane!" Isabella and Pintus cried back in unison.

Pintus knelt at Mr. Cane's side. "They're gone!" he whispered, face glowing. "Queen Lamia is dead. We've taken back the castle. We're safe!"

He reached out and clutched Mr. Cane's hand. It was cold. "Let's get you to the hospital wing."

Mr. Cane looked as though someone had lifted a thousand pounds off of his shoulders. "F-Free!" he gasped. "F-Free! S-Safe! P-Pintus, the c-castle and the kingdom will never be able to repay you, you w-wonderful, c-clever boy!"

"It – it was Isabella, too, and Carole Sa–" He stopped. "Mother. It was Isabella and Mother too!"

Mr. Cane managed to beam at them before groaning at the pain it caused.

"You need the doctors. Guards! Come in here – Mr. Cane needs the hospital wing!"

"Yes, Your Highness," the guards murmured in unison.

They stepped out of the bathroom while Mr. Cane was carried out of the room and to the hospital wing. Pintus knew, with a lurch in his stomach, what he needed to do next.

As Pintus walked down the curving staircase with Isabella and Carole Sanderson, he could almost hear, like a distant nightmare, the clanging of armor, he could almost see the guards closing in behind them. Pintus walked numbly down, floor after floor, dreading the moment when they would reach the bottom. Pintus knew what was coming, but it didn't quite seem real.

Pintus could already see the trampled, limp figure of Darold. He stopped hard. He felt as though someone had punched him hard in the chest.

"Go on," Carole Sanderson whispered.

Pintus and Isabella slowly reached Darold's side. Pintus struggled to breathe normally. Isabella knelt down beside Darold. Pintus did the same. He focused on Isabella's white hand as she traced the button on her dead friend's cloak over and over again.

Then, with a deep shaky breath, Pintus forced himself to look up at Darold's face. Isabella was slowly and carefully closing his eyes with her slender index finger. It made his face look much different. Smooth. Relaxed. Peaceful.

Pintus took a deep breath. "He's happy now," he said to Isabella, voice cracking halfway through the sentence. She nodded. That was all he needed to say.

As the guards carried him away to be buried, Pintus felt something lift inside of him.

He was thinking about when he could get out of the castle to assure the merchants that they could safely reopen all the stores and shops when suddenly Pintus heard a distant rumbling noise. A million fears gripped him. Could the kingdom be rebelling against their hard-won triumph? Could Queen Lamia have possibly survived the fall and was now banging against the entrance with all of her minions? Somehow, though, despite his shallow fears, Pintus knew that wasn't it.

Isabella's eyes widened. "Come on, this way, quick!" She snatched her brother's hand and led him up the many flights of stairs back to the room leading to the balcony. Carole Sanderson hurried after them. The sound was growing louder now – the very castle was trembling from the growing, rumbling noise coming from outside.

Isabella released Pintus's hand and ran out onto the balcony. A smile slowly spread over her face. "Pintus," she said, "come over here."

Pintus walked slowly towards the doorframe. His heart was thudding in his chest. He stopped at the open door, looking questioningly at Isabella. She motioned for him to come out onto the balcony. That was when he realized that the entire kingdom's population was outside the castle, looking up at the balcony, and chanting:

Prince. Prince. Prince. Prince.

Pintus looked quickly at Carole Sanderson. She gave him a smile and a nod. "It's yours now."

Isabella ran from the balcony back inside to Pintus. She nudged him. "Go on, Pintus," she said. "Your kingdom is waiting."

A beam of weak sunlight broke through the clouds, streamed down upon the kingdom, and shone upon the balcony. The crisp air swirled with bits of drifting snow as Prince Pintus stepped onto the stained wooden balcony to greet his kingdom.

About the Author

Kelsey Marlett is the twelve-year-old award winning author of her short story "Healing Eruption" and "The Closet Broomstick."

For more information on and from Kelsey Marlett, visit her website to get an inside look at her work, read some free short stories she's written, and learn about her as a person as well as an author.

Kelseydaymarlett.weebly.com

14349868R00131

Made in the USA
Charleston, SC
06 September 2012